AJESH SHARMA

A Couple of Choices

SloWord

This novel is entirely a work of fiction. The names, characters and incidents portrayed in it are the work of the author's imagination. Any resemblance to actual persons, living or dead, events or localities is entirely coincidental.

Ajesh Sharma asserts the moral right to be identified as the author of this work.

Second edition

ISBN: 978-0-99-592711-7

This book was professionally typeset on Reedsy.
Find out more at reedsy.com

Contents

What readers have said

"incredibly layered and complex"

"If you like to pause, listen, reflect on the spaces between the words, if you like to let your imagination take over and co-create with the author this one IS for you"

"Beautifully written with cheeky and witty dialogues."

"A good, fun, clean book with some quotable quotes"

"can teach anybody a thing or two about relationships"

"if you haven't read this one, do not miss it at any cost"

"an absolute must read in case relationships fascinate you"

"A gripping human interest story that had me turning page after page"

"Was great because it touched on the things that people go through but don't like to talk about"

Preface to the Second Edition

I've had to rewrite large portions of this Preface to the Second Edition. Why, you ask?

Well, I showed a proof copy to a couple of friends and they said I seemed to be apologizing for writing this book, or play.

I have no intention of apologizing for it.

It came out the way it did. Possibly, for a very good reason. I think it works as it is and works quite well. If I didn't think it worked, I wouldn't have put it out there for you to ignore.

I didn't set out to write this story as you see it today. Especially, I did not think I was going to use the format in which you see it today. It started life as a half-baked short story, with strong overtones of sadness. It lit a spark in the couple of readers who read that early story. Somewhere in the months after that short story came to be, it morphed into a play.

When I first completed it, I sought the advice of a few people about this story. I poked around in groups where readers and writers talked about books.

Most people I spoke with, who had experience of the publishing world, warned me that writing it in a play format would not go down well with the large bulk of those who read. For this reason, I was going to struggle to find any publishers to take it on.

They were right.

I ignored all the advice I received and released it as a play, because I believe it works as a play. I visualized it as a sort of movie, and I captured it as I saw it in my head.

I believe I am right.

The feedback to the story is generally positive. A weather reporter could have described sales as "mild with sunny breaks", however. Some readers found the story philosophical. Some saw it as utterly realistic. Some reported that it taught valuable lessons about life. Some didn't think the characters should have responded the way they do.

They are all, probably, right.

We can, and do, and should, take away something from everything we read. Every story is viewed, as it should be, through the lens of personal opinion and experiences, and there are no wrong or right feelings.

A few readers stopped reading soon after they realized it was a play. Some did not get started at all for that reason! Regrettably, however, some readers pointed out flaws in editing and formatting.

Those who pointed out typographical errors were right, and are, hereby, commended on their keenness, and very much appreciated.

This edition is about formatting for print and ebook. It is not about changing the story in any way.

Now, about the story itself.

The story is, likely, not an entirely unknown one.

The complexity of balancing "self" and "other" is difficult. It is not easy to dissect, break down, and act upon our life to reach emotional, financial and mental comfort.

We make choices as we go through life, and every choice has some consequence or result. Sometimes we refuse to make choices for ourselves and leave it to life to have its way with us.

Very often, we have choices thrust upon us because we are surrounded by people making choices of their own. Sometimes, circumstances leave us with choices that are not really choices.

We may choose safety over conflict, conflict over introspection, aggression as a form of defence. Some leave it all to fate, in a sort of hopelessness born of desperation and the inability to cope.

At the end of it all, we are faced with our own self, as shaped by the life we have lived; a life itself shaped by all the choices that envelop us in their tight embrace.

I do believe that to deal with the constant change, introspection should be a constant theme in our lives.

From that perspective, this story is about reflection, choosing with care, adjusting, adapting and understanding who we are, and identifying and recognizing the people who care for us.

Thank you all for your continued patience, support and feedback.

Ajesh Sharma, 2024

Foreword to the first edition

This work owes its existence to a couple of very special people.

Over seven years ago, I was suddenly blessed with oodles of spare time. My wife, Rita, told me to use it, wisely and well, in the pursuit of writing. "Why not try your hand at writing? You've been whining about it for years now".

Decades of togetherness have trained me to follow her instinct, intuition and instructions, usually with mixed results, so you now know whom to blame for this story.

For allowing me to mope around the house over the countless months while this story turned my head to sludge and for her patience, love and indulgence over the years, I cannot thank her enough.

She will remain, always, the one choice I will never regret.

When I first sent Anjana Dutt a barely formed short story, she responded with encouraging noises over the internet. She then took over the role of artistic bludgeon, delicately beating me over the head to develop this. Acting as sounding board throughout, she helped me edit and fix my abysmal storytelling.

Last, but by no means least, she conceived and designed the beautiful cover by the simple expedient of bullying me into taking multiple photographs, up and down and in an out and all around my house, until she had the ones that suited her wonderful design.

I'm still not sure how this turned from a short story to a novella to this play format, but I do hope you enjoy the story. It gave me a lot of trouble, so you better! Thank you!

Ajesh Sharma, 2017

Cast of Characters

Alex : A middle aged writer

Linda : His friendly agent

Phyllis : Alex's estranged wife

Stephanie : Alex's assistant

Mark : Alex and Phyllis' son

Andrea : Mark's younger sister

ACT I - Scene 1

The stage is split into two areas. On the left is a covered patio, with a large sitting area. At the back, white French windows lead into the kitchen. Past this door, the house continues at right angles to itself. A door in the wall at right leads into Alex's study. This door is closed.

Enter Alex and Linda from the kitchen door.

LINDA: So! Today is the lucky day, then!

ALEX: Yep, and you had to insist on coming over, didn't you?

Linda is a cool, slim, assured, middle-aged lady. She is dressed in a pale blue fitted shirt and dark blue pants with a slim leopard-skin belt. She carries a medium sized bag, which is stylishly dark and functional. There is no trace of motherliness about her, but she is not cold and harsh.

Alex is dressed in blue jeans and a shirt with blue, green and black checks on a white background. On his feet are dark blue suede shoes. He is a lean middle-aged man with greying hair.

LINDA: Yes, I wanted to see if you were ok. What time does she get in?

ALEX: Uh, her plane gets in around noon. She made me promise I wouldn't go and pick her up. Slightly delayed, it says, so I can spare you half an hour.

Talk quick!

LINDA: I'm curious. Why is she coming here after so many years?

ALEX: To see how I'm doing?

LINDA: I don't think so. It's gotta be something pretty important. Why else would she suddenly call and say she's on her way? All the way from the East Coast? It's very odd. I don't like it. But, get me a coffee and sit down. We need to understand this. Plus, I got news for you!

ALEX: Black, one sugar? When are you going to give up on the sugar?

LINDA: I need it to deal with the likes of you!

She walks around the patio, looking out into the distance in front.

LINDA: You know, every time I see those vineyards and those hills, I can't help but think what an absolute lucky devil you are. You have this incredibly lovely house, with those lovely views.

ALEX: Thanks to you, I suppose, my dear bloodsucker.

LINDA: And don't you forget it, my boy!

ALEX: Enjoy the view while I get your coffee.

Alex goes out into the kitchen. Linda surveys the patio.

The seating area is shaded by wood beams that can be adjusted to control the sunlight. The crossbeams are embedded with lights. Seating consists of two large armchairs, placed close to each other, facing the front with a side table on either side of them. Two identical sofas with a low table in the center complete a neat and

3

symmetrical conversation group. The sofas look soft and comfortable with colourful cushions to brighten them up.

Linda wanders around and stops at the door to Alex's study. She tries the handle gently and finds it locked. She backs away, stands there shaking her head slowly.

LINDA: What have you got in there, Alex? How many memories do you have locked inside?

Alex comes in with two mugs of coffee.

ALEX: Linda, refresh my memory. When was the last time you walked in and didn't say "I have news for you"?

LINDA: This time it really is news. And must you use these mugs?

He chuckles. He places the mugs on the low table. He sits down in the left chair and indicates the seat next to him. She comes around to sit on the sofa to his right.

ALEX: And it always is! And I must. These are the remnants from an ancient civilization that went to wrack and ruin and these are all that remain. They're major archaeological relics! You should be proud I let you use them.

She sips her coffee and peers at him over her mug.

LINDA: Huh! Did she buy these for you or did you buy them together? Or are these the mugs you used to drink your first coffee together?

Alex grimaces.

ALEX: You're so damn cynical! I suppose being a literary agent did that? You know, turned you into a soulless vulture preying on the egos and emotional needs of talented but impoverished writers.

LINDA: You mean you still believe in the romantic notion of writers living in dark garrets with but a solitary sputtering candle to provide warmth and light? Quite a garret you have here! Who designed it for you?

She waves her arm around the patio and towards the house.

ALEX: It's all mine. I dreamed it all up. I'm good at dreaming. I've had lots of practice.

LINDA: Oh yeah?

ALEX: Yeah. The only problem with dreaming is that sometimes dreams become reality and you realize you're in a nightmare and you want to wake up, but it's too late, you're in it and the only way out is for you to slap yourself out of bed and drink coffee.

LINDA: Must you always talk like this? I don't get it. Is it a habit or some sort of a psychological compulsion? I don't understand what you're saying most of the time! I suppose that glib mockery stems from some deep-rooted insecurity.

ALEX: Yeah, maybe it does.

LINDA: You were so quiet when we first met and not quite so flippant. It's getting worse by the day, you know.

ALEX: You think so?

LINDA: Yep. Maybe senility is creeping up on you. Or insanity.

ALEX: Insanity! I used to think I was quite sane, until I started mingling with other people. That's when I realized that they were all quite crazy and so was I.

LINDA: Oh really?

ALEX: Oh yes, I'm as normal as anyone else. You're crazy, too, you know. But you're one of them and I'm one of me. And it's a battle that goes back and forth. It's a matter of who is crazier at any given moment in time and who is crazier more often, how long the intervals are between moments of craziness. It's a game of marginal wins and losses.

LINDA: Enough! I didn't come here to receive a lecture.

ALEX: Yes, you came here to wangle something out of me. As always!

LINDA: You don't look different.

ALEX: Should I?

LINDA: I... somehow I thought there'd be something different today. Though, you're more talkative than usual. I suppose the thought of meeting her is making you nervous?

ALEX: It is different. I don't plan to write a thing today...

He holds up his hand as she starts to say something.

ALEX: And, I told Stephanie I'm taking the rest of the week off. I don't want any distractions.

LINDA: The rest of the week? Off?

ALEX: Yes. I'm taking some time off.

LINDA: Some time off! From what are you taking some time off? Are you really taking some time off? Or have the rest of the days been off and now you're going on?

ALEX: Didn't you say you had news for me?

LINDA: Avoiding the subject? You? Wow!

ALEX: What?

LINDA: You really are scared, aren't you?

ALEX: Scared?

LINDA: You are!

ALEX: Why should I be scared?

LINDA: You tell me!

ALEX: Oh, all right! Apprehensive, I would say, not scared.

LINDA: Whatever you say…

ALEX: Can we get to the news?

LINDA: I'd like to meet her.

ALEX: Well, you're not going to. I don't want anyone around when she gets here.

LINDA: It seems I've seen so much of her already and I feel I should see if the real thing matches the imagined. She's in those books of yours, isn't she?

ALEX: Whatever you believe is ok with me.

7

LINDA: I've known you now for what, eight years or so? We've been through four books together. I'm always the first to really read them, you know?

ALEX: Yes, I know. You've been a good girl. You're still not meeting her.

LINDA: I feel I should. I want to know.

ALEX: You want to know? What do you want to know? You already know all there is to know.

LINDA: Not all.

ALEX: Look Linda. She was my wife, once upon a time…she is still my wife. We split up. We both moved on. I quit my job. Wrote a few books. You helped me get them out there.

LINDA: That's the short version.

ALEX: Yes, you're responsible for all this.

He waves his hand around.

LINDA: No, you did it. I like your patio, but I prefer my kitchens small and country. Not the ultra-modern gadget-filled thing you have back there. This is more my style, warm and comfortable, though the adjustable crossbeam shades, up there, are a bit gimmicky. Why couldn't you have an awning like everyone else?

ALEX: Maybe it's a guy thing, the gadget thing.

LINDA: And you're a macho guy? No, I don't think so.

He clutches his heart.

ALEX: Argghh, that hurts! How could you Linda?

She smacks him on the shoulder.

LINDA: You're a sentimental softy, all marshmallow inside with a nutty crust to protect you.

ALEX: Stop it! Did you come over to insult me or give me some news?

LINDA: It's not an insult. The news is women like crusty, cynical men who are soft marshmallow inside. Haven't your book sales told you anything?

ALEX: And that's another thing - would you please stop signing me up for all these women's reading club speaking things? They all ask the same questions.

LINDA: You need them. They buy your books.

ALEX: So they want their pound of flesh? Can't I do a podcast?

LINDA: Running away still?

Alex speaks bitterly.

ALEX: I wish I was. I suppose you're here about yet another dinner at the Ladies of San Benito Cultural Association or something?

LINDA: Why are you so rude?

ALEX: I told you. I'm not a nice guy.

LINDA: No. You're not being very nice right now. How long will you hide?

ALEX: I'm not in hiding. I live here. This house isn't moving. Anyone who knows me and where I live can find me easily here. If people wanted to, they could find me quite easily.

LINDA: Oh, please… no self-pity and bitterness.

She shushes him, as he is about to speak.

LINDA: You don't think that living alone in this massive place with not even a dog for company is not hiding? You moved in 3 years ago and since then I've seen you become quieter and quieter. Do you still talk to yourself?

ALEX: No, I don't. I never did. Not anymore.

She shakes her head.

LINDA: Ok, back to what I want. I want to meet her. How long is she staying?

ALEX: Staying? Overnight, I suppose. She hates multiple stops and the next available and feasible non-stop back east is tomorrow evening.

LINDA: Have you got her bedroom all set up?

ALEX: Yes. She is not sharing my bedroom.

LINDA: Why did you guys never get a divorce? Everyone else does.

ALEX: I suppose it just didn't occur to us. Marriage was always an afterthought for us…. me. We were just very good friends. We… I… didn't think of it as being married.

LINDA: Oh. What did you think it was then?

ALEX: Friends should not get married.

LINDA: Why, mister know-it-all?

ALEX: Marriage kills friendship. Friendship kills sex. Sex, eventually, kills marriage. It's a bloodbath.

LINDA: What a way you have with words! Any old combination of words will do to hide behind an honest answer. Does that even make sense?

ALEX: It is an honest answer. It's what I know and believe to be true. I know your book club ladies won't understand that. They keep asking questions about it and I don't think they understand my answers. Actually, I'm not sure even I understand myself, so I can't blame the poor things.

LINDA: I think they want to reform you! But there is a story you haven't told us yet, Al, my friend! I suppose the next book will have some of it?

ALEX: Oh please, not Al. I hate being called Al.

LINDA: How did you guys meet? The real story....

ALEX: We just drifted into it. I suppose she must have given some signals that I picked up or vice versa. Who knows?

LINDA: I think you just don't pay attention.

ALEX: I must have picked up something, I suppose.

LINDA: Hmm. So why did Phyllis leave? Do you expect her to come back?

ALEX: She did not leave. I did. If anyone were coming back, it would be me.

LINDA: Sure... you left. Did you, really? Do you believe, honestly, that you have left it all behind? Those four books you sold so many copies of, are they fiction, as you claim them to be?

ALEX: My work is fiction. Of course, all writers draw upon stories people tell them. People tell you anecdotes from their lives when they find out you're a writer. Authors even use things that they themselves have experienced. Then the writing process takes all these little anecdotes and stitches them together into a coherent, I hope, story. So what is fiction really, but reality, someone's reality, retold?

She waits for him to finish.

LINDA: You're talking to me, Alex. Me. Linda. Your agent. You're not speaking to a room full of fans, the book club ladies you were disparaging a moment ago.

ALEX: I know, Linda. I'm telling you. You've known me now for 8, 10 years, been through my books, you've read things that didn't make it to the books. I get it. You understand me, you think. But do you?

LINDA: Well, we'll find out in your next "work of fiction"

She makes a quote gesture.

LINDA: It will be in there somewhere, won't it?

She looks at him, quizzing him. He looks away and hurriedly checks his phone.

ALEX: Hell, look at the time. I gotta go. Come for dinner then. Be here at 7:30. You can meet her then. Hopefully, that will stop your prying. And then you and Stephanie can compare notes.

LINDA: What time are you leaving for the airport?

ALEX: Around 11:00.

LINDA: I thought you said she made you promise not to pick her up?

He is caught out. He grins a sheepish smile.

ALEX: Well, I think it would be rude not to. I don't want her trying to find her own way here.....

LINDA: You little softy, you male chauvinist pig!

He tries to protest, but she brushes it off.

LINDA: 7:30 PM. I'll be back! And you cleverly did not answer my question, Al! By the way, you're speaking to the Santa Rita Literary Ladies Club on the 23rd of next month. They're giving you lunch, so put on your usual charm.

As he reacts to the news, she gets up, picks up her things then turns to Alex. The lines on her face lighten as she stares at him. He stares back and shrugs a 'what?' She shakes her head. He walks to the kitchen door with her.

ALEX: I'll let you out.

LINDA: Wow! You never show me out. You are rattled! Don't worry, I know my way out. You'd better hurry to the airport.

She exits out of the kitchen door. Alex comes hurrying back.

ALEX: Damn, I should be heading out soon.

He walks to the sofas and surveys the patio. He fusses over the cushions, fluffing them up and replacing them carefully. He takes a key from his pocket, unlocks the door to his study and enters.

It is a well-furnished and warmly lit room. The rear walls are lined with bookshelves crowded with books. At rear left is an overstuffed chair, set at an angle with a lamp that loops up over it. Next to it is a comfortable sofa. Against the right wall is a window. Under this is Alex's L-shaped desk. One arm runs at right angles to the window and carries a laptop and monitor. The other arm faces the door.

Alex has a comfortable swivel chair encased in overstuffed leather. Two smaller visitors' chairs sit with their backs to the door, sideways to the audience. Walls not given up to bookshelves, are hung with watercolour paintings of cheerful landscapes and old narrow lanes. One or two bright cushions on the sofas give the room added dashes of colour.

Alex walks around the room, moves a cushion or two, fidgets with the items on the desk.

He goes over to a large piece of furniture hidden under a dust cover at front left. He removes the sheet to reveal a large overstuffed leather reclining chair-and-a-half. He dusts a speck of dust off the chair and stands there, inspecting it.

Finally, goes back to his desk, sits down, leaning forward and staring ahead at the chair he has just uncovered. He gives up after a while and leans back in his chair looking up at the ceiling, before shaking himself and picking up the phone from his desk.

ALEX: What time is it? Time to be leaving, son! Come on, Al, my boy! Get moving! Don't want to keep her standing there.

His eyes go the chair again. He walks over to the chair and stands looking down at it.

ALEX: You're soft, Al, very soft...

ACT I - Scene 2

Alex and Phyllis are seated on the patio.

Alex is in the left chair and Phyllis on the sofa at right. There are plates on the table in front of them. She has a wineglass in front of her with a bottom third of white wine in it. He has a long tumbler of lemonade.

Phyllis is about Alex's age, of medium height and slim, with a warm and bright look about her. There is an air of competence around her. She is dressed in blue jeans and a scarlet blouse, tucked in. On her feet she wears comfortable sandals, with heels that are comfortable and neither too high nor too low.

ALEX: So there we are. Getting over the flight?

PHYLLIS: Yes. Thanks so much for coming to pick me up and taking care of the rental car. You really shouldn't have!

ALEX: Nah! Don't worry about it. So what did you think of the drive up here?

PHYLLIS: It's so pretty! I'm glad you came to pick me up! It gave me the chance to admire it. If I'd been driving I wouldn't have been able to pay attention to it so much.

ALEX: I do like it. I see your point about missing the best part of the drive if

15

you're driving. You think you would've been able make your way up on your own? No trouble with the directions?

PHYLLIS: You're fishing for compliments! No, you always prided yourself on your directions and I'm sure these would have been perfect!

Her smile takes the sting out of it.

ALEX: No, no, that's not what I meant. I do tend to get carried away a bit.

PHYLLIS: Don't you feel you're a little cut off?

ALEX: Not really, no. I like it here. It's quiet. I can cut in and out of communication and work quietly without disturbances. I get to be in control...

PHYLLIS: You should get a dog. A big, happy dog. Like a lab or a retriever.

ALEX: Ah yeah.... not really feeling I want to take care of a dog just yet. But I do like Labs and Retrievers. I think they're big and warm, very friendly dogs.

PHYLLIS: Well, I don't think you have to worry about size. You have plenty of room here for a couple of big dogs.

She picks up her wine and takes a sip.

PHYLLIS: What wine is this?

ALEX: That's a Riesling, from grapes that came from the vineyard over there. They specialize in sweetish whites, Riesling, mostly and some Zinfandel as well. It's not a very big vineyard.

He points.

PHYLLIS: This is a lovely patio. Great view!

ALEX: I like sitting out here. It's usually nice out, no matter the season.

She appraises him over her glass.

PHYLLIS: So you made it! You're a famous author! How does it feel?

ALEX: It feels …uh… ok! There are, as with anything, pluses and minuses. There is a cost to everything. You win somewhere and lose something. You gain a yard, lose a foot or two. You have tea but no scones or biscuits but no coffee. Or, you have tea when you need coffee. Life is a funny thing. Not haha funny. Not all the time. Sometimes, it can get very weird indeed. Someone asked me what my books were really about and I said "Life. Life is weird. I write about life. That probably makes me weird, even though it's a logical fallacy of some kind, I think!" As usual, I lost them.

He chuckles quietly.

PHYLLIS: You lost me there too. I suppose it's another one of your carefully crafted sayings meant to confuse people.

ALEX: What you're actually saying is I like to confuse people to make myself feel superior. That I am quite insecure, right?

PHYLLIS: Does it matter what I think? We've lived apart for some time now. I live out there and you live here.

There is a pause. He takes a sip from the lemonade, not meeting her eyes.

PHYLLIS: Are you working on another one? When is that coming out?

ALEX: Oh, I don't know, it's a hard grind getting this one down. It seems like

I said everything I wanted to say in the ones already out there, so I'm going back to being lazy and taking my time. It's going to be different from the others, I think.

PHYLLIS: I read the first two as soon as they came out. You've got a gift.

ALEX: I think when you feel strongly about something it's easier to put it out there.

PHYLLIS: Yes, maybe that's true. But you've always wanted to write…you were always going on about it.

ALEX: Guilty as charged. Ah, but wait. So you haven't read the other two?

PHYLLIS: I didn't mean that. Of course, I read them all.

There is a slight accent on the 'of course', which Alex does not fail to notice.

Phyllis gets up and walks away gazing out over the valley in front. Alex waits, not saying anything. Phyllis takes her time, scanning the vista.

PHYLLIS: I wanted to talk to you about a couple of things.

She turns around to Alex who is watching her carefully. He indicates the sofa.

ALEX: Don't be shy; just help yourself to more wine or whatever.

She waves away the offer and sits down on the left sofa. He leans back.

PHYLLIS: This is difficult, but I wanted to speak with you directly. I did not want to do this over the phone.

ALEX: Hey, I know that Andrea is engaged. I assume this has something to do with that?

PHYLLIS: She wants you to attend the wedding and I wanted to know how you felt about it.

ALEX: Hmm, I didn't know she wanted me to attend.

PHYLLIS: Of course, she'd like you to attend. How could you think she wouldn't?

ALEX: Phyll, 5 years ago, she did not seem keen on telling people she had a father.

PHYLLIS: 5 years ago, Andrea was a young mixed up girl, Alex.

ALEX: So is that her excuse? Or is that your reason?

PHYLLIS: Reason, excuse, whatever! Does it matter?

ALEX: It does to me. Does she really want me to be there? Does she want her Dad there? Or does she want to keep up appearances? Or is it the successful author she wants to show off? You know, Andrea has always been focused on herself.

PHYLLIS: That's not fair. You know that she cares, deeply. She's always wanted you to give her attention and you never had time for her. You know, you've always made everything sound like it's about you. And it wasn't always. You needed to stop thinking about yourself so much and feel things, let yourself feel.

He is silent. He leans forward, head downcast.

ALEX: Did she send you? Or was it your idea?

19

PHYLLIS: It was my idea. The kids, both, they care for you, they always have. You were just not able to see it. And I know you've always cared deeply for them and they were not able to see it, too. I've talked to both of them and….

He cuts her off.

ALEX: Sorry, I know all that. But they are adults and they should start behaving like adults. I was always being told I did not treat them as adults and I'm not going to treat them like kids now. They need to grow up and stop expecting the advantage both ways.

She sits back and stares at him. He waits.

PHYLLIS: So what do you want to do? Do you want to ignore them and their existence, cut yourself off?

ALEX: What do you think I want?

PHYLLIS: An apology? If she were to call you and apologise, would that help?

ALEX: Phyll, an apology from her is meaningless in this context.

PHYLLIS: I don't understand that. Just now it seemed like you were blaming Andrea.

ALEX: Phyll, you have to understand this. I don't really want anything from anyone anymore. I've got past all that.

PHYLLIS: What if I told you that I wanted you to attend the wedding?

ALEX: I'd ask you, "Why?"

PHYLLIS: Andrea is your daughter. She loves you and I know you love her.

Isn't that enough?

ALEX: Love isn't as strong as they make it out to be. Don't believe the novelists and writers who tell you that love conquers all. Love does not always quell fear. In some cases, it loads fear with loathing, with regret, with indifference, resignation and separation. Love got us here, Phyll, arguing about kids, our kids, our lives, our reasons, our excuses and our choices.

PHYLLIS: Still making speeches, I see.

ALEX: I never used to. When I started, it ended our relationship.

PHYLLIS: So what does that say about me?

ALEX: Figure it out. You're a smart woman, much smarter, some would argue, than I.

PHYLLIS: I don't want to go back to the past.

ALEX: Yes, I can see that. You've moved on, I see, and I hope you're happy. You certainly looked happy at Mark's wedding. At least, in the photos I saw, because I never got an invitation to that wedding. Thanks for the photographs, by the way. At least I did get to see my son on his wedding day. A couple of months later, but ...

He waves his hands.

PHYLLIS: I didn't think you'd be happy to attend.

ALEX: Assuming again? How come you didn't think that I would want to be invited to my son's wedding? Though in this case, you may have been right. I'd certainly not have been the happiest person there.

21

PHYLLIS: So would you have come? If I'd invited you?

ALEX: I don't know. I probably would have come. Did Mark ask about me?

PHYLLIS: Would it have mattered?

ALEX: Whether Mark wanted me at his wedding? Whether my son wanted me at his wedding?

For the first time we see anger in his face.

ALEX: You really do not understand, do you?

PHYLLIS: I suppose there is no point in talking about the past.

ALEX: Yes, there is, actually. The past brings you to the present and shapes your future. You have to understand the past, work on your present and prepare for the future. I sure as hell think there is a point in talking about the past.

PHYLLIS: So what do we do then? Dredge up all the debates from all those years ago? How often have we talked about this? If you'd stop being so blind to the others around you, you'd see a little bit of how others see it.

ALEX: If you'd stop thinking that I wanted to ignore people, you'd see a little bit of how I see it. You lived on assumptions on how I feel. You've made that the basis of your relationship. You never bothered to listen to what I had to say. You just brushed it off as some useless rubbish. You didn't try to see my point of view. It was all about how I should behave. It wasn't about how I felt.

PHYLLIS: How you felt? You never told me how you felt.

ALEX: There was never a moment to tell you anything. There was never a moment when you weren't busy with something or the other...kids, work, other family members, friends. I was at the end of the list.

PHYLLIS: You know that I never...

Alex cuts her off.

ALEX: Sorry... you know what? I've changed my mind. I do not wish to talk about the past. I used to say I live without regret. Now I say, I wish had no regrets. It is a strong man who can actually live without regret.

PHYLLIS: Regret? I think you talked about regret a lot, like you said, but I think you did regret a lot of things. Do you regret marrying me?

ALEX: No. You know that. I will never regret that. You were the best thing to happen to me at the time.

PHYLLIS: I do. I regret wasting that time. I regret wasting your time. You could have done what you wanted, maybe.

ALEX: That's not something we should be saying. I didn't know what I wanted. Or rather, I didn't know what I would want later. People change.

PHYLLIS: People don't change, really. I think, at their very core they don't. You just stopped being yourself.

ALEX: I stopped being myself? Who did I become then?

PHYLLIS: I don't know how to say it. You just became very cold and very aloof. You shut yourself up somewhere. I don't know. I can't say it like you can.

ALEX: How ... uh.. Let me think, how do I say this? Uh. Ok, look, don't you

23

think that you had something to do with it? Don't you think that you "shut yourself up"?

PHYLLIS: Maybe. I don't know. I guess I did too, but I had things to look after, the kids, the house.

ALEX: Yes. I get that. And I didn't figure in that list of things, did I? What I said before…

PHYLLIS: What did you expect me to do?

ALEX: I think this conversation is going exactly like all the other conversations in the past. So, let me look forward then. As you said, we can't turn time back, unless we can somehow make the earth spin the other way, very quickly, what, 12 times 365 days, give or take a leap day or two.

PHYLLIS: Alex, I didn't come here to bring up all that. I'm sorry about shutting you out of Mark's wedding. I… I don't want that to happen again. I came here to ask you to please come for Andrea's wedding. I want you to give her away. It's a very simple thing.

ALEX: Simple? You think you can just call me and say you want to come over and then all you want is a simple yes to a request like this? Are you kidding me?

PHYLLIS: Well, I wanted to see you personally. I know I messed up by not talking to you about Mark's wedding. I didn't want to make the same mistake again. Andrea needs someone to give her away.

ALEX: Does she want this? Don't you have anyone else to do that?

PHYLLIS: I don't have anyone else, Alex. I know you may find that hard to believe but that's the way it is. It is either you, or I don't know…

ALEX: So you're stuck without me. Or stuck with me. Is that it? Why don't you ask Andrea to call me? I want to talk to her. I want to hear what she really wants. I'm really tired of the kids using you as their mouthpiece. I'm never sure whether what I'm hearing is what you want or they want. This has to stop.

PHYLLIS: They're scared of you. They don't want to hurt you. You have to know that. You do know that.

ALEX: Phyllis, you know exactly what I'm saying. You know more about me before I know it myself. You've always known. I think you've pandered to them. Even now you are protecting them and I don't think they need protection. Not from me. Frankly, I find it insulting. They need to have a direct line to me. That's the reason we're having this conversation. That's the reason you...

He stops, shakes his head and sits back.

PHYLLIS: So this is not going anywhere, then?

ALEX: Short answer? No!

PHYLLIS: You've grown harder. Much meaner, more determined. You really are not going to budge on this, are you? You're not going to come to the wedding? You refuse to give Andy away? You won't do this for her? For me?

He smiles at her.

ALEX: You're making assumptions again. Look, I don't do debates anymore. I never liked them. When I did get into angry debates how much damage did that cause? You're here, sitting in my house, seeing me after years, you still want me to do things. You still want to tell me what I should do. You still don't care how I feel. You just want me to do things.

25

They sit back and stare at each other. The silence seems to last a long time.

PHYLLIS: Do you think I don't trust you? Is that it? Trust comes from doing things. You have to build trust. Trust is earned, not given.

ALEX: And we're back, ladies and gentlemen! Yes, Phyll, you didn't trust me. You didn't trust yourself. Do you know that?

PHYLLIS: What?

ALEX: The issue isn't whether you trust me. The issue is you didn't …don't… trust yourself. Which is why you're so wound up, trying to do the right thing.

PHYLLIS: Someone has to think about the risks.

ALEX: But when will you let it go? The kids have grown up and left home. I've grown up and left home. Who are you going to mistrust now? There's only you left.

PHYLLIS: Yes. There's just me. But, you know, to love someone is to learn who you are first. To love yourself. That's been the problem for both of us. We didn't love ourselves. We didn't know ourselves. Yet, we expected the other person to know us. How can anyone else know you better than you know yourself?

ALEX: Yes. That's true.

PHYLLIS: We were too young, Alex. We were too scared, scared of hurting the other person. And look where we are now… Listen. I'll ask Andrea to call you, since that's what you want. But will you do this… For me? It's the last thing I'll ask you to do for me.

Alex leans forward and puts a hand out on her arm.

ALEX: Phyll, why don't you just not meddle? Let her decide for herself what she wants to do. Don't tell her what she should or should not do.

PHYLLIS: I worry about her, Alex.

ALEX: She's grown up, now Phyll. Does she know you're coming up to see me?

She shakes her head. He throws his hands up, gets up and stalks away to the left behind her.

ALEX: You came all the way here to see me. To tell me what I should do. You've decided what Andrea wants. You've decided for her.

PHYLLIS: I haven't decided anything.

He comes swiftly around back to face her, leaning on the back of his chair.

ALEX: You need to let it go, Phyll. We all have to move on.

PHYLLIS: Move on? That's easily said.

ALEX: Some things are meant to be. Some things you don't need come easily to you. Some things you think you desperately need, but do you really? We have to work out what works and what doesn't.

PHYLLIS: I'm tired of thinking so much.

ALEX: Look Phyll, I've tried not to look backwards with regret. Sometimes, yes, I've fallen prey to regret, but there's always been the desire to move on and find a way out, that's got me out of that kind of mood. Regret and guilt are useless feelings that gain you nothing. You have a problem, you figure a way out. Sometimes, a way out is the only way out.

PHYLLIS: Still playing with words.

ALEX: It's the truth I live by now. There comes a time when you have to stop running and make a stand. I made my stand and so I live here all by myself. I have some income, enough to afford this house and some nice things for myself. I do still enjoy writing; I even enjoy the talks, the publicity jaunts.

PHYLLIS: I thought you'd enjoy those talking events.

ALEX: It is nice to be recognized for what I've done. I get to go out and meet lots of people. I get to stand there and talk about lots of stuff with strangers. They all want to know how I feel, what I felt when I wrote the books, why I wrote them, are they based on my personal life. Personal questions they really should not be asking me.

PHYLLIS: So what do you tell them?

ALEX: I tell them that it's a story. Read it and figure out what it means to you, understand your own reaction, your feelings to it, in your personal context. Don't expect me to tell you how you should feel. But they do, Phyll, they want me to tell them. And I can't. Or won't.

He pauses. He sits down again in the chair.

ALEX: And I won't tell you how you should feel. You will have to work it out yourself.

PHYLLIS: So, you've grown up now?

ALEX: Yes, if you will, I've grown up. I have no one to share my fame and wealth with and sometimes, yes, it does bother me. I know now that I will not have that anymore. I've come to terms with my life, Phyll. If you ask me whether I'm happy, I'll have to say, I'm as happy as I can be, given the circumstances. That is enough.

PHYLLIS: So you're happy, really happy?

She leans forward, searching his face, with genuine interest.

ALEX: As happy as I can be. What about you, though? Are you happy?

She pauses and sits back.

PHYLLIS: I'm well looked after. I have everything I need. You've made sure of that. I never thanked you for it.

ALEX: You didn't answer my question. But let it go. You're not the type to answer such questions. Let's just agree that you'll let Andrea figure it out. If you wish, you can tell her you spoke with me and I do love her a lot. I always have. Tell her I said so and she can call me anytime she wants.

PHYLLIS: You didn't answer my question either, you know. I was hoping I'd get you guys to... get together. I wanted to talk to you, Alex. I wanted to see you... see if you're doing ok.

ALEX: It is good to see you, Phyll. You know that. I have always ... listen, just let Andrea be. Give her some space to make up her own mind. Please. She'll surprise you, I think.

PHYLLIS: I'll have to take your advice. I did take it, quite often, you know...

ALEX: Yes, I do know. I haven't forgotten what it was like to be with you, Phyll. We were good together. We had some great times. Hey, we'll always have Vienna!

She smiles a genuine smile.

PHYLLIS: There's nothing like a cliché... That is one of the good memories. We could have had more...

They sit in silence.

PHYLLIS: This conversation did not go the way I expected, so I suppose I'm not that good at working on you, Alex, like you used to say. Don't have you wrapped around my finger anymore...

ALEX: You expected me to give in. We both said the other changed, but Phyll, do people really change? We're still the same people we were when we first got together. No?

She nods her head slowly.

PHYLLIS: We matured, we were young and foolish... life gave us lessons and we failed some of the courses.

Her cellphone rings. She fishes it out and answers it.

PHYLLIS: Hi, Andy. What's happened? I'm away for a couple of days. Where? I came to visit your dad. Yes, I know. Andy, calm down. I'll be back the day after. No, everything is fine. Nothing has happened. Take it easy. No, you can go ahead as planned. You don't need me to be there. Just make sure that you get what you really want. Remember, this is one day... yes, if you have any doubts don't confirm anything. Just tell them you'll think about it and call back to confirm. We can talk later. Yes, I'm back tomorrow night. Ok, talk to you later then. Bye.

She shuts down phone.

PHYLLIS: That was Andrea. She's fussing about flowers and music. Apparently, Dave sent her a playlist and it doesn't match her idea of music suitable for a wedding... so she came over and found I wasn't there.

ALEX: Sounds like Andy.

In complete sync: They both pick up their glasses, take a sip, put the glass back on the table, lean back, stretch their legs out in front of them.

ACT I - Scene 3

It is the evening of the same day. Alex and Linda are standing at the bar.

He is wearing charcoal grey slacks and a white shirt with little blue cornflowers printed all over it. His sleeves are rolled up past his wrist. His shirt is tucked in. Linda has changed into a dress, a dark, simple A-line sheath that fits her beautifully. She is wearing dangling silver earrings and a matching chain around her neck.

ALEX: Well, here we are. Do you mind hanging on for a bit? I'll be right back.

He goes out into the kitchen and comes back with a tray of hors d'oeuvres, which he puts down on the cocktail table and goes out. He comes back in again this time carrying two bottles of wine. He puts them on the bar. He looks around. Linda watches him, her head cocked.

ALEX: Ok, what am I missing? Wine, glasses, beer in the fridge, though no one is going to have any. God, I hope I know what I'm doing. Stop talking to yourself, Al!

LINDA: You're fussing!

ALEX: I'm not!

LINDA: Oh yes, you are! You're a worried man. Well, so how has it gone so far? I hope you've been nice!

ALEX: I'm always nice! It's the one thing I am. All those reading club ladies say so. The internet is full of comments about how nice I am. The internet is never wrong. If it says I'm nice, I'm nice!

LINDA: Modesty becomes you, but, occasionally, you should blow your own trumpet.

Alex grins.

ALEX: Sounds like a plan. OK! From now on, I shall be modest always.

Phyllis enters from the kitchen door. She has changed into dark pedal-pusher slacks and a black silk popover blouse with white and pink floral patterns.

PHYLLIS: Especially when you have so much to be modest about.

Linda turns towards Phyllis.

LINDA: Ah! He needs people like you to drop things on his head! You must be Phyllis.

PHYLLIS: Well, I must, mustn't I? Be Phyllis, I mean, unless you're used to seeing strange women in his house.

LINDA: Oh yeah, he has these wild orgies every Friday evening. Why don't you stay over for the weekend and check it out for yourself?

ALEX: What? Orgies? Here? Why hasn't anyone told me? Have you been renting this place out, Linda? It must be after I go to bed.

Alex turns to Phyllis.

ALEX: I go to bed at 8PM sharp.

PHYLLIS: Really? 8PM? You expect me to believe that? You never went to bed before midnight!

LINDA: You see what he's done? He's managed to draw you off into that discussion, thus leaving behind the orgy scene.

PHYLLIS: You know, I think, 8PM isn't that farfetched, really. An orgy certainly is. I don't think Alex likes crowds much.

ALEX: You don't, do you? Well, Linda is right. Why should I lie? I have groupies hanging around all the time. I kept them away today by telling them I was coming down with the flu. Naturally, they wouldn't want to catch the flu from me, flu being contagious and all that. And them being in close proximity to me, draped, yes, draped all over me, would naturally cause them to feel exposed. And no one likes the flu, do they?

Linda and Phyllis look at each other and then him, waiting for him to finish.

LINDA: Right, that's settled it, then!

PHYLLIS: Yep, 8PM it is.

They shake hands ceremoniously over the agreement while they appraise each other.

ALEX: Nice to see you get along. Who wants a drink? White wine for both?

Phyllis takes the big armchair on left. Linda takes the sofa on left. Alex goes back to the bar, pours out white wines for them. He comes back to them on the left and is confused to see Phyllis in his chair.

LINDA: I think he likes that chair, the one you're sitting in. It's his spot you're in.

PHYLLIS: Well, he won't mind if I take it for a while. Will you?

She looks at him - puts out a hand to him. He shrugs and hands them both a glass. Phyllis turns back to Linda. Alex goes back to the bar for his glass.

PHYLLIS: So, you've known him all this time?

LINDA: Yes, he came here with a computer and a large document on it. We met at one of those writers' clubs. When he found out I was an agent he tried to show me the document.

Alex comes back around and sits in the sofa on right.

ALEX: And she automatically assumed that I was hitting on her.

LINDA: Well, one can never be sure. In this business, it's best not to go back to see some guys "etchings".

Phyllis nods.

PHYLLIS: Or his "manuscript". So what happened next?

ALEX: She gave me her business card and asked me to email her my manuscript.

PHYLLIS: So, he sent you a Non-Disclosure Agreement...

Linda almost chokes over her wine.

LINDA: Yes! That's what I got.

ALEX: Well, in this business you can't be too careful. You don't want to be sending your work out to just any female calling herself a literary agent.

LINDA: Touché! Well, played, my friend, well played!

Alex raises his glass to her.

PHYLLIS: So then you signed it? Or did you send it to a lawyer?

ALEX: Ha ha ha!!! She's got you, Linda! I told you she was bright as a pin!

LINDA: Of course! I don't sign just anything. Well, anyway, a month or so later, I did see the manuscript.

PHYLLIS: And the rest is history?

ALEX: Not quite. She made me re-write 80% of the bloody thing!

LINDA: Yes, he was a good boy. He did fix some of the weaker spots. Then we took it out to get a publisher interested.

ALEX: That was quite an experience…. I had no idea publishers were such nitpickers.

PHYLLIS: Oh, and you're not, I suppose?

LINDA: Gotcha!! Once we got the deal prepared, he took ages to read and understand it.

PHYLLIS: And then questioned the wording of every clause. Yup, that sounds like Alex all right!

ALEX: I wanted to make sure that my words would go out to my public as I wrote them. That they would go out in the media of my choice and that I had full control over the rights. After all, my hard work, my talent, my gift to the people should get the treatment it deserves.

PHYLLIS: He can be slightly pompous. I'm sorry... I tried.

LINDA: Yes, now that you mention it, I have felt sometimes that he gets above himself.

PHYLLIS: Like now. Alex, calm down. We get your joke, most people won't. So pick your audience.

ALEX: Well, you guys got it. So I did pick my audience, didn't I?

LINDA: He has a slight tendency towards glibness. Did he always talk like that?

PHYLLIS: He was pretty sober when we first met, but then I noticed he always had something clever to say.

ALEX: That's what you loved about me... Hey, listen I gotta go check on a few things in the kitchen. Be back in a bit. You guys doing all right for drinks? Bar's back there, if you need anything. Just holler if you can't find something...

He gets up and goes out into the kitchen.

Phyllis and Linda sit back. There is a renewed sense of appraisal in the air. Each waits for the other to speak.

LINDA: You're wondering about me. And him.

PHYLLIS: Uh, not really.

She's not very convincing.

LINDA: Well, let me clear that up. Alex and I are business partners, nothing more. He writes. I sell. We've never been more than that.

Phyllis recovers herself.

PHYLLIS: Well, I didn't mean to pry. And really we've been separated now for nearly 10 years, so I'd be surprised if he hadn't moved on.

LINDA: Would you? I mean, be surprised?

PHYLLIS: Ten years is a long time.

LINDA: Did you move on?

PHYLLIS: Well, I've got used to living alone and looking after myself. I quit working a couple of years ago. I help out here and there. I guess I've moved on.

LINDA: You avoided the real question.

PHYLLIS: Well, no, to answer your question.

LINDA: Really? Why ?

PHYLLIS: Uh…it just isn't high on my list. I find most of them shallow and sorely lacking a sense of humor.

LINDA: Been spoilt, huh? Living with that Alex… You like his sense of humor, do you?

PHYLLIS: Yes, he was funny. Still is, I think. But with us… he became quiet and a little bitter. Then he wasn't fun anymore. He just sounded annoyed all the time.

LINDA: I gathered that he left and not you?

PHYLLIS: I think we'd both left, in our own way. He physically left, yes.

LINDA: Was it hard?

PHYLLIS: I suppose it was. The first few days were difficult.

LINDA: You know what I mean. Was it hard for you to realize that he had made the decision? That he'd changed so much?

PHYLLIS: I guess it was a shock to see... know that he'd reached snapping point. We'd been together a long time. We were just very good friends. Then we drifted away from each other. It was like one of us had moved to another city, but we kept in touch and met up occasionally. We didn't realize anything serious was happening. Then the meet-ups became fewer and we grew further apart. There was always so much going on; kids, work, house, things.

LINDA: And then?

PHYLLIS: Then one day it looked like we were in opposite corners of the world. The world we'd made for ourselves didn't exist anymore. We built it and then we destroyed it from inside.

LINDA: And you didn't even know it....

PHYLLIS: That's about right. It crept up on us, slowly took us over, then suddenly one day it was over. He was very quiet. He gets very quiet and scary when he's really, really reached the end. He just said, "I have to go away. It's best if I do. I'll figure something out and let you know what's next."

LINDA: And then he left.

PHYLLIS: Just like that.

She falls silent.

LINDA: What about the house, kids, money etc?

PHYLLIS: He just packed and left. Then I found out he'd quit his job. All our money was in joint accounts anyway. He hadn't changed a thing.

LINDA: He just disappeared?

PHYLLIS: He called a few weeks later. Something about some bank stuff. I asked him where he was. He said he'd moved across the country. It was a very short, business-like discussion.

LINDA: How did you guys meet? You both must have been quite young?

PHYLLIS: Yes. We were in university together. We were hanging out in the crowd, doing the usual things; the strange parties in strange houses at strange times. We got along. As I said, he can be quite funny and very charming. He had a way with him even then. He wasn't like the other guys. There was an element of naïveté about him.

LINDA: He is sharp though.

PHYLLIS: Oh yeah! Don't get me wrong. He is quite strong-willed when he wants to be. It's just that he doesn't take strong positions first crack out of the box. At the same time, some of our friends used to say that he comes across as someone who makes up his mind very quickly.

LINDA: That's weird.

PHYLLIS: Yes, it's a bit of a paradox.

LINDA: How did you guys decide to get together?

PHYLLIS: I suppose we just drifted in. There wasn't a conscious thing. You know how it goes. We used to take long walks. We were able to talk a lot to each other. There was a time when I must have wanted it never to stop. It didn't seem that we would ever stop talking, walking together.

LINDA: And then?

PHYLLIS: I don't know how it happened. He was his usual self, chatting on about what he liked, what he'd like to be.

LINDA: Was being a writer on the list?

PHYLLIS: He liked reading. He didn't think about writing. He wasn't really sure what he wanted to be. Back in the day, it was about getting a job and rising through the corporate ranks. But even then....

LINDA: Yes?

PHYLLIS: He was pretty clear about what his space would look like. He knew what his house would look like – all glass, steel, mirrors, modern looking.

LINDA: Not this traditional style?

Waves her hand at the house and patio.

PHYLLIS: That came later. Back then he wanted a modern look. He wanted a separate office for him. Just for him, he said, with a big desk, a comfortable chair, just for him, where he could lock himself up.

LINDA: And he described this to you?

Linda's tone is gentle.

PHYLLIS: Yes, and while he was talking, this …. this thought popped into my head "and a big chair in the corner for me to cuddle up in and watch you work." Then he jumped on that and I realized, I'd spoken out loud and then we realized that…

She sits there, staring ahead.

LINDA: Wow! That's quite a story!

PHYLLIS: I guess so. I don't know… it was so different. It seems so far away now.

LINDA: When it changed, you never made any attempt to make a clean break?

PHYLLIS: That's what I find odd. We'd both agreed that clean breaks are the best. We made a few together; moving between cities, leaving places and people behind. You know, getting on with our own lives.

Takes a deep breath.

PHYLLIS: It didn't occur to either of us to file for divorce. Neither of us knew what to do. Eventually, it just kind of stayed that way. We never made the clean break.

LINDA: Yes, I asked him about it. He said the same thing. That it never occurred to either of you. You chose not to file for divorce. Why?

The question is suddenly sharp and direct. Phyllis is a little taken aback at the abruptness. She shrugs.

LINDA: You must know. Both of you must know. He's not the type to do things without a reason or a plan. And from what I've read and heard, neither are you. So.... why did you guys never think of a divorce?

PHYLLIS: I haven't really thought about that. I'm sure there is a reasonable answer to it. Somewhere...

LINDA: I think, you kids need to come clean, with yourselves and with each other. Don't you think this has gone on long enough?

PHYLLIS: What's your interest in this?

LINDA: I hate to see him the way he is.

PHYLLIS: Do you love him? Are you in love with him?

LINDA: Look, I've known him for a few years now. And I still don't know him. I don't know him the way you know him. And I never will. He doesn't think I.... you should have seen him back then. He was someone who was very quiet but with a strangely aggressive tension in him. Over the years he's become less aggressive but quieter and quieter. It doesn't seem right, somehow. It seems time is killing something inside him in some ways. I don't think he has much left to write and ... no wait, I think he no longer wants to write. I think he's done. And it worries me.

Phyllis doesn't say anything.

LINDA: I can see you thinking "she's worried about her business". Phyllis, I can tell you, honestly, I don't care about that. I've made my pile, I have others who will churn out their 100,000 words a year and I can sell them and I'll still get on. No. It's not that.

PHYLLIS: You love him that much?

LINDA: He's not meant for me, Phyllis. Look around you. What do you see? Do you recognize anything?

PHYLLIS: Yes, I've noticed it. What do you think I am? Of course, I've known before I came here what I would find. He's talked about it for years. Everything he has here is almost exactly as he described it over the years. The years spent dreaming, the days he would sit there talking about when he would make enough to get what he wanted. He knew, in great detail. He had it all in his head, from the colour of the walls to the furniture. It was his most annoying habit.

LINDA: So you know what I mean, then. He's created his dream here, in the most excruciating detail. I find that disturbing. Don't you?

PHYLLIS: He had his dreams and now he's living it.

LINDA: Is he Phyllis? Is he?

PHYLLIS: I... One would assume so.

LINDA: He has an office he won't let anyone into. Did you know that? He's never allowed anyone in. I haven't been in. His editor, Stephanie, too, has never been allowed in. He is careful to keep it locked behind him. I tried it this morning, his door, and, not for the first time... Locked.

PHYLLIS: You mean?

LINDA: I think he's waiting, Phyllis.

Linda gets up and walks over to kitchen door and peers in. She walks back. She comes back around to face Phyllis.

LINDA: Do you still want him back?

Alex comes in.

ALEX: Ok, we're all set! But I have some news for you, Phyll. Your flight for tomorrow is cancelled. Weather delays... You're stuck here for another day.

He notices the tension and stops.

ALEX: What happened? Has Linda been bugging you, Phyll? We can send her home, if she has...

PHYLLIS: What? Oh no! Alex, what are they saying about the next flight? I have to go back. Andrea ... the wedding... there's so much work to be done. Are they rebooking me? I have to call them.

ALEX: Hang on a sec, I have an idea. Since you're here anyway and you haven't seen this part of the world much, why don't you just stay on for another couple of days and I'll show you around?

LINDA: What about my book?

ALEX: Oh, damn the book. I'm entitled to a few days off, sometime. What do you say, Phyll?

PHYLLIS: Quite a proposition! Should I?

He waits, neck out, head cocked, eyebrows raised.

LINDA: You should take him up on the offer. Stay and enjoy our part of the country for a bit.

PHYLLIS: Hmm, alright, I'll call Andrea and let her know. Then I have to call the airline about the flights. And, I'll need to go get some stuff because I only packed for an overnight trip.

ALEX: I called the airline already. Tomorrow, we go shopping to get you your stuff. Then to a little place I know for lunch.

LINDA: You mean you've already changed the flights? You…

Alex shrugs. Phyllis shakes her head.

ACT II - Scene 1

It is the morning after. Phyllis is seated in Alex's chair on the patio. She's dressed in jeans and a t-shirt, her feet are bare. On the table in front of her is a coffee mug.

Alex comes in.

ALEX: So how did Andy take it last night, when you told her you were going to stay here for a couple days?

He sits down in the other chair.

PHYLLIS: She's freaking out. I'm sorry, Alex, she's decided to come over to see what's going on. She just sent me a text, she'll be here tomorrow morning. I'm really sorry.

ALEX: Ahh … don't worry! It's ok. It will be good to see her. It's been too long.

PHYLLIS: She has a list for everything; playlists, guest lists, and other lists. She really is very upset. Promise me, you won't be upset when she comes, Alex. I don't want…

He cuts her off.

ALEX: It's ok, Phyll. I'll be nice, don't worry.

He chuckles.

ALEX: I'd like to see those lists! I'm sure I'd have ideas of my own.

PHYLLIS: I'm sure. But let her deal with it.

ALEX: What I've always said…

PHYLLIS: Though, I think, you were being selfish when you said that.

He refuses the bait.

ALEX: Selfish? You mean I wanted them to go away and stop bothering me? I suppose that's true.

PHYLLIS: You admit it, finally!

ALEX: I prefer to think of it as enlightened parenthood. Give them a leg up and help them think for themselves.

PHYLLIS: That's one way to look at it.

ALEX: Never mind now… It's done, we're here now.

PHYLLIS: I see you haven't lost your touch with those omelets. It's been ages since I had those.

ALEX: It's like riding a bicycle. I haven't made them in years!

PHYLLIS: Well, it certainly helped bring back some memories.

She holds her mug up.

PHYLLIS: You still have these? When did we get these; our fifth anniversary, no?

ALEX: Fifth, yes. It's a shame to throw perfectly usable mugs out. There is something comfortable about them, like old slippers.

PHYLLIS: I'm sure you can get better ones now.

ALEX: Nah, I went looking and gave up. The new ones just don't feel right. They're either too small or they're humongous. These are just the right size.

PHYLLIS: I still have the rest of them, too. There's nothing like good coffee. This is good, very nice coffee.

ALEX: You like it? It's a blend I mix up from three different varieties I buy. I use 1/3rd mix of each. I like the balance. I see you've taken to having it black now.

PHYLLIS: Yes, milk, cream just became unnecessary.

ALEX: Hey listen, I was wondering. Do you want to drive down and see the sunset over the ocean? We can make a picnic dinner out of it.

PHYLLIS: Hmm, that sounds nice.

ALEX: I have to get some stuff done today, first though. Stephanie insists she wants me to look at a few things and apparently it has to be done in person.

PHYLLIS: That's ok. I'll just laze around meanwhile. It's been a while since I had nothing to do.

ALEX: It's a bit of a change for you, isn't it?

Doorbell rings.

ALEX: Stephanie, I think.

He goes out and comes back in with Stephanie.

Stephanie is 30-something, young enough to be easy-going and old enough to be assured. Dressed in slacks and a colourful printed blouse, she advances upon Phyllis with a big smile and outstretched hand. They shake hands.

STEPHANIE: Hi! I'm Stephanie. I'm so glad to finally meet you. Alex doesn't talk about you much. I mean...uh...

PHYLLIS: It's ok. I know what you mean.

ALEX: Stephanie has way too many questions and I get bored easily. You can be pretty darn nosy, Stephanie! And that's the reason you just had to come over today... no?

PHYLLIS: I'm sure he doesn't mean it that way, my dear.

STEPHANIE: No, I know what he means. I'm used to his ways now. Don't forget I read all those rough drafts.

She has a quiet laugh, with just a giggle at the end.

PHYLLIS: So you're the first person to see them, then?

STEPHANIE: Yes, quite a privilege! I'm thrilled to work with him. He's quite the celebrity! I have a group of friends who do similar work for other writers and they're all very jealous of me.

ALEX: Yes, yes. We have work to do Stephanie.

STEPHANIE: Actually, I think I get to see a side of him no one does. I'm pretty lucky actually. I have quite a picture of him. For one, he isn't as grumpy as he makes himself out to be.

ALEX: Based on the fictional scribbling I give you to fix. Yes, um, wow. You're privileged.

STEPHANIE: Ah, but, you see, you can hide, but what you try to hide reveals as much about you as what you reveal.

ALEX: Wow! One of your own or did you pick it up somewhere?

STEPHANIE: One of my own! Would you like it to use it for your stories? I'll give it to you, for a price.

ALEX: Hmm, wonderful thought. But no thanks, I'll pass.

PHYLLIS: You haven't asked the price, Alex.

STEPHANIE: Well, it's been a real pleasure to meet you. I can see that Alex is raring to get on with work.

PHYLLIS: Thank you. How long have you been working with him?

STEPHANIE: Oh, about 3 years now. He writes really good stuff. Some of it comes out of the text when we edit. I've been editing for about 9 or 10 years now and working with him has been the most fun!

ALEX: Thanks! I aim to provide fun. The books are purely secondary, a bonus. Now can we get on with it?

PHYLLIS: You sound like you're in a hurry, Alex.

ALEX: No, no. It's just that we have to finish that piece there and if we want to go out later this evening then I want to finish it as quickly as possible.

STEPHANIE: Oh, are you going out tonight? I thought you were heading back tomorrow?

PHYLLIS: No, I moved the flights. This has been a nice trip, so I'm staying for another couple of days.

ALEX: It's my irresistible charm.

PHYLLIS: Yes, well… I'll go read for a while up in my room then. Nice meeting you, Stephanie.

STEPHANIE: Bye. Lovely meeting you. I hope I'll see you again soon.

Phyllis goes out.

ACT II - Scene 2

Alex is in his chair on the patio. He has his legs stretched out and eyes closed. Phyllis comes in.

PHYLLIS: I heard Stephanie leave. You guys are done? Are you ok? You look tired?

ALEX: Uh no. I mean, yeah, I'm ok.

PHYLLIS: Are you sure?

ALEX: Yeah, I'm ok. Just a little tired. That Stephanie is young and has energy and I'm just getting old I think.

PHYLLIS: And I'm just as old as you… just a couple of old people. Old friends.

ALEX: Yeah, old friends.

He takes a deep breath.

ALEX: I need a long cold drink.

PHYLLIS: Alex, I….

She stops.

PHYLLIS: I wanted to see your study. I meant to ask earlier.

ALEX: In there. It's just a room with a desk. I like to be able to shut myself off.

PHYLLIS: Linda mentioned you won't let anyone in. If you don't want me to see it, it's fine, too.

Alex gets up and walks towards the door connecting to his office. He takes out a key from his pocket and unlocks the door. He opens the door wide and bows elaborately to usher her in.

ALEX: I've known you longer than I've known anyone and, as you said, we're old friends. The oldest I know really well ... and the best. Please!

Phyllis slowly walks through the door into Alex's inner office. He follows her in.

PHYLLIS: Hmm, so the magic happens here. Where those fancy words come out?

ALEX: Sort of. Sometimes I go out to the patio and work for a bit. But mostly I write in here. I like it. It is how I've always wanted it.

PHYLLIS: Oh, that's a lot of books. What have you got?

She walks around the room, checking the books on the shelf. She turns around walks back and sees the chair in the corner. She stiffens and turns around towards him. He is sitting at his desk watching her.

PHYLLIS: Yes, I do see. It's almost exactly like you described it. I'm glad you were able to get what you wanted.

ALEX: It's just a room. Not everything I ever wanted. It's quiet and gives me a chance to be alone with myself

PHYLLIS: Yes. I can see that it is a very personal space.

ALEX: So you've seen the place now. What do you think?

PHYLLIS: It's … lovely, I like it. Thank you for letting me in.

ALEX: You're always welcome here. Any time, Phyll. Don't need to ask.

PHYLLIS: Alex, that dinner picnic….

She breaks off.

ALEX: Yep, still on. If you're still up for it, that is.

He stares into her face. She shakes her head, slowly.

PHYLLIS: No, I think I'll have to give it a miss. Hey, uh. Can I borrow a car?
I think I'll just go out for a bit. I just need some alone time, so I'll just get out
of the way for a bit… I'm sorry.

He comes around to where she is standing, dragging keys off the table in passing.

ALEX: Of course. Here, take my car. Let me know when you're done. I'll
rustle up something here for dinner.

PHYLLIS: Don't worry about dinner. I just don't feel like a sunset picnic… I'm
sorry.

She looks at him. He stares back. Neither one smiles.

ALEX: Sure. That has the house key on it too. Where are you going to go?

PHYLLIS: I don't know. I'll just go sit in a coffee shop or something. Let's see.

ALEX: If you take a left as you come out of the drive, then drive about 5 to 6 minutes and take a right, it'll take you to the village center. It's only about a 10 minute drive away. You'll find coffee shops and stores there.

PHYLLIS: Left out of the house and a right?

ALEX: Yes. Call me if you get lost. You sure you don't want me to drive you down to the town?

PHYLLIS: I just need to be alone for a bit, Alex.

ALEX: I understand. Take your time.

PHYLLIS: Thank you. I'm sorry I ruined your picnic.

ALEX: Hey, don't worry. I'll keep dinner for you, anyway. Just in case.

She stares at him for a few seconds then turns abruptly and goes out, into the patio and out through the kitchen door. Alex follows her out to the patio, then goes back to his desk and sits there, staring up at the ceiling, his feet on his desk.

ACT II - Scene 3

It is the next day. Alex comes in, followed by Phyllis, Andrea and Mark.

Andrea is in her twenties, dressed in jeans and knitted top, soft, low-heeled grey pumps on her feet.

Mark is a couple of years older, tall and well dressed in khakis and a checked shirt, with a white t-shirt showing at the collar and loafers on his feet.

ALEX: Well, here we are. How's everyone doing?

PHYLLIS: I don't understand why you guys came all the way.

Mark turns to Alex, ignores Phyllis.

MARK: Nice place! I like this patio. She made me come. She was worried sick about Mom being away. I didn't want her haring off on her own.

ANDREA: Mom, you said you were going for an overnight trip! But then you changed your flights...and no word on when you're coming back.

PHYLLIS: I told you. I called to explain. Anyway, I am booked day after tomorrow now.

Alex whips around to stare at her.

ANDREA: I don't understand any of this. Dad, you tell me what's going on.

ALEX: It's lovely to see you, too, my dear. Still hyper, I see.

ANDREA: I thought you'd forgotten all about us.

ALEX: Oh, yes, I remember now. I left you guys to fend for yourself, didn't I?

ANDREA: You walked away from us, dad!

ALEX: You've done all right, though, haven't you? You've had your mom looking after you. You're all grown up now. Mark, already married and on his way to being a successful lawyer, and you've not done too badly yourself, have you?

PHYLLIS: Everyone just calm down, please? Alex, please...

Alex shrugs.

ALEX: I'm not raising my voice and I'm calm.

ANDREA: Neither am I, mom.

MARK: And I didn't say a word.

PHYLLIS: Good, let's keep it that way. Alex... they're here now. Can we just sit down and talk about this?

ALEX: Sure. Look. I am very glad to see you. Mark, I'm sorry I could not make it to your wedding. Things got a little out of hand at the last minute...

Phyllis interrupts.

PHYLLIS: The truth is, Mark, I did not send him an invite. It is my mistake. It was something I felt then I was not comfortable about. I should have told you earlier.

Alex turns to her in exasperation.

ALEX: He didn't have to know the gory details! Why'd you do that?

PHYLLIS: It's time he knew.

MARK: It's all right, Mom, I knew all along. When he didn't show up, I knew you'd probably told him not to come, or did not tell him about the wedding.

ALEX: Well, there's his legal training coming out. Glad to know it wasn't wasted.

ANDREA: But that's quite stupid! Why would you do that, Mom? He needed to be there.

ALEX: Must you always be so quick to make judgments? Your mother also has feelings, you do realize? You can't call her stupid.

PHYLLIS: It was not right. I apologise for it.

ANDREA: But that is just sillier. What's the point of apologising now?

MARK: You need to see the bigger picture, Andy, see other people's point of view sometimes. Just slow down and count to 10 before you say anything and while you're counting - think!

PHYLLIS: It was a very difficult time for me... us all.

ANDREA: If I were you, I ...

MARK: If I were you, I'd shut up.

ANDREA: Oh keep quiet. I hate the calm way you take things. For once in a while will you take a stand?

ALEX: It isn't necessary for him to take a stand. He doesn't need to take a stand. It's not that dire, Andy. It's over, gone, done, my dear. Whatever you do now, is not going to change the past.

ANDREA: And you're just like him! All don't worry, stay calm. I hate that! For once in a while can you be passionate about something?

PHYLLIS: Andrea, stop it. You cannot talk to your father like that. You have no idea what you're saying!

ALEX: You came here to talk to your mom and find out what's going on, right? Ok, then, talk to her. Mark, you want a drink? And what can I get you two, Phyll, Andy?

PHYLLIS: I'm ok. Andrea, Mark, you've come off that flight, you must be tired…

MARK: I'll go with Dad and get something. Wine?

ANDREA: Not wine - anything cool?

ALEX: Lemonade?

She shrugs. Mark and Alex exit into the kitchen. Andrea and Phyllis remain as they are. Phyllis seated on the couch, Andrea standing.

ANDREA: I don't get it, Mom. What are you doing here? You just left without saying anything. The wedding is 4 months away, there's so much to do.

PHYLLIS: Andrea, I know this wedding means a lot to you. It is your wedding and I want it to be your wedding, not mine. I've tried to help. Sometimes I think I've got too involved. I want you to take charge and make up your own mind about your wedding.

ANDREA: But I need you, Mom! You want me to take on everything? The decorations, flowers, music and a million other things still need to be decided!

PHYLLIS: I want you to take care of them. Don't worry, I'll be there to help, but I want you to lead. You decide, you research. If there's help you need to work something out, call me. You and Dave have to decide for yourselves.

ANDREA: Call you? Are you staying on here with Dad? Are you getting back together? I don't understand!

PHYLLIS: No, as I told you, I'm going back home in a couple of days. But I still want you to take care of things. Only call me if you need help. I'm too tired to take ownership.

ANDREA: Uncle Lester called last Tuesday. He assumed he was giving me away. I told him yes. I can't imagine Dad will be coming. You won't let him.

PHYLLIS: What do you mean by that? Do you want him there? It's not about me letting anyone do or not do anything.

ANDREA: You're always in charge, Mom. Everyone knows that. Dad will do whatever you tell him to.

PHYLLIS: First of all, you have to decide if you want him there. Next, if you want him there, tell him so. You have to tell him, not me. Go direct.

Enter Alex and Mark, each carrying two glasses of lemonade.

61

ALEX: Here you are. Oh, just wanted to check on dinner.. Shall we go out ? What would you guys like to eat? Any preferences? I know a couple of nice, quiet places where they know me.

He bares his teeth in an exaggerated caricature of a grin.

He hands a glass to Phyllis, who indicates the table in front of her. Andrea takes a glass but does not sit. She walks away around Phyllis so she's standing right behind her. Alex sits down in his chair and Mark takes the couch across from Phyllis.

MARK: The perks of fame, eh, Dad! Nice!

PHYLLIS: Can we get some take out? I don't know if these two are too tired to go out.

MARK: I'm ok to go out.

ANDREA: I don't care one way or the other. Dad will want to go out too. You're outvoted, Mom.

PHYLLIS: Alex, will you call ahead?

ALEX: Don't worry; I'll take care of it.

PHYLLIS: Where are they going to sleep?

MARK: Stop fussing, mom.

ALEX: I've got spare bedrooms. No problems there.

PHYLLIS: Are you sure?

She looks at him, very serious.

ANDREA: Mom, if he says it's ok, it's ok! Can we get on?

Alex waves at Phyllis.

ALEX: No issue there. There's a bedroom free, next to the one you're using and there's another opposite it. Two free bedrooms, two people.

He counts off on his fingers, as he speaks.

PHYLLIS: Andrea, you use the one next to mine and Mark can use the other.

MARK: It's ok, Mom! No one really is worried about that. We'll figure it out.

ANDREA: How can you just sit there! Talking about food and dinner and... and... sleeping arrangements. Like nothing happened? You just go away with some stupid message and then I don't see you for 10 years. Now you pretend as if everything is ok?

ALEX: Isn't everything ok? You're through college with a Masters, you have a good job, you're getting married to a good, solid guy who loves you and presumably you love him too. Mark is already married and settled. You've got your mom to thank for being there always. Have you ever said thank you? To her?

ANDREA: Don't make this about me! How dare you? You're the one at fault!

PHYLLIS: Andrea, sit down! And stop talking about fault. I've told you no one person is ever at fault when it comes to relationships.

ANDREA: But, Mom..

MARK: Sit down, Andrea. Mom is right.

ALEX: If I may, please, remind me, how old were you when I left?

ANDREA: 18... I was only 18.

MARK: Only.

ANDREA: You stay out of this!

PHYLLIS: Andrea, you need to sit down.

MARK: I notice that you were quite ok with me tagging along. Exactly whose idea was it for me to come on this trip? She wouldn't even let me nap on the flight.

ANDREA: I can't help it if you decided to come.

MARK: Oh really? Well, let me jog your memory. You called me and said "we need to go over and find out what's going on". We... If I remember right, you were quite worked up about it.

ALEX: Mark, Andrea, both of you need to take it easy. I'm not really sure what everyone is up to. Should we start from the beginning? Take a deep breath, everyone.

Andrea comes around and sits down heavily next to Phyllis, leaning forward. Mark sips his drink, legs stretched out and relaxed.

PHYLLIS: Before anyone says anything, I want you to hear what I have to say. I came here for a reason.

MARK: Yes, mom, I would like to hear what you have to say.

ANDREA: Why did you come? To see dad? I'm still confused...

ALEX: I think instead of focusing on why she came, we should focus on why you guys came. Mark, were you really just supporting Andrea or did you also want to come?

MARK: I...

ANDREA: Yes, I also wondered how you agreed so easily.

MARK: I definitely did not want you heading over on your own, Andy. And I also thought it would be a good time to figure out what's happening with everyone.

ANDREA: Look, I'm trying to plan a wedding and when Mom just disappeared like that I got worried.

ALEX: What were you worried about? The wedding or mom?

PHYLLIS: Alex... Stop it, please!

ALEX: I think Phyll; the time has come for young Andrea here to start fessing up. You're getting married in a few weeks, Andy, you're supposed to be grown up. But I don't see anything more than a disgruntled 17 year old. You're making this about you, aren't you? You're worried that your precious wedding will be somehow ruined?

PHYLLIS: Alex! Stop it!

ANDREA: I was worried about Mom, Dad! I don't know what you mean... yes, I am getting married but, how can Mom just disappear like that?

ALEX: Surely, as an adult, she can decide what she wants to do? Are you trying to dictate to her what she can and cannot do?

PHYLLIS: Andrea, I came here to talk to your father.

MARK & ANDREA: Why?

ALEX: She came to ask me to attend your wedding, Andrea.

MARK: I don't think so, Dad.

ANDREA: What?

MARK: Think about it, Andrea. Do you believe she would have come over just to ask Dad to attend your wedding? She could have just called...

ALEX: I don't think it really matters why she came, does it?

MARK: Oh, I think it does and you know it too.

ALEX: Ok. I'm getting a little annoyed now. Andy, you come barging in here, yelling and shouting and from what I can tell you're worried about making your wedding a perfect day. For you. Have you ever stopped to think about how everyone else feels? How about that guy you're marrying? Does he get a say? Have you stopped to consider what he thinks about the wedding?

PHYLLIS: Alex, please!

MARK: Dad does have a point there, Mom.

ALEX: And Mark. You look comfortable there. At least you're not whining like Andrea. Thank god for that! But, here's a question for you, Mark. What made you drop everything and come here with Andrea? Was it really about giving her support? Trying to be big brother? What does your wife have to say about it? Does she know that you're here? How come you didn't bring her along?

Mark is still leaning back, but he draws his ankles back. He starts to say something. Alex cuts him off.

ALEX: I'll say this. At least Andrea is herself. She's all about herself, but that's her. I know that. You on the other hand, came here looking for me. What is it that you want? Why did you really come here?

PHYLLIS: Alex, I think...

Mark stops her.

MARK: Sorry, Mom, I think Dad has a valid point. We did all come barging into his house.

PHYLLIS: No one came barging in.

MARK: Dad, this is why I came. I wanted to talk to you. Face to face. I want to know. Why did you leave?

ALEX: My reasons for leaving? You want to know why I left?

PHYLLIS: Is there any point at all in trying to go back to that? I don't think there is any value in that.

MARK: I think there is. Dad's told us often enough that to move forward you have to understand the past and evaluate the present.

ALEX: The question really is this: What is it that you want? In the future. Looking for answers for the sake of answers is meaningless without defining your future expectation.

ANDREA: Ok, everyone stop! I just want to know one thing. Dad, are you coming for my wedding, or no?

ALEX: Do you want me to?

Phyllis, Mark and Andrea all three speak together.

PHYLLIS: Yes.

MARK: He will.

ANDREA: What?

MARK: Look, it's quite simple. Andrea doesn't really care. She'd rather be walking down the aisle with Dad, but isn't tied to it. I don't care if you do or not. Mom is the only one who really cares. And she cares for two reasons. One, because you missed my wedding and, I think, she believes she made a mistake there and is trying to fix it. Secondly, she wants to do it for Andrea.

Everyone falls silent. Alex gets up and walks away to the door. He stops at the kitchen door and looks back at the three of them. He turns back and walks over to face the three of them.

PHYLLIS: Andrea, Mark, you…

MARK: Am I wrong, Mom? You know I'm not.

PHYLLIS: Yes. I did not tell him about your wedding. Did you? Did you ask me why then?

MARK: No. I did not because you did not want him there, did you? And I didn't want to make you uncomfortable. Anyway, Dad had been away for some time and I believed he did not want anything to do with us. Am I right?

ANDREA: I don't understand, how you can say that I don't care….

Alex cuts off her off with a wave of his hand.

ALEX: Andrea, Mark is right. You need to stop and think before you start speaking.

ANDREA: I don't understand why we're going around in circles. I just want simple answers to some simple questions.

ALEX: Go ahead, ask.

ANDREA: Are you coming for my wedding?

ALEX: Do you want me to be there?

ANDREA: Yes. I want you to give me away.

ALEX: Ok. Done! What else?

ANDREA: That's it for now from me.

MARK: I think that's over simplifying things.

ANDREA: I'm simple minded, ok? You can keep your damn legal training. I just want to know. I don't give a damn what happened and why it happened. I just want simple answers to simple questions.

PHYLLIS: Mark, Andy, let's keep it here for now. You guys need to get back and get on. Andrea, you now know your dad is coming for the wedding. Leave it at that and you can continue with the prep. Mark, I'm not sure what you told the folks at the firm and how long you can stay away from work. I think, you need to get back to work.

MARK: How come she gets her answers and I don't? Spoilt brat!

Andrea puts her tongue out at him.

ALEX: Ok that's settled. Now what are we doing for dinner? Why don't we all go out and find a nice, quiet place?

ANDREA: I need to change.

PHYLLIS: Yes, me, too. Leave in half an hour? Alex, you decide. Do we need reservations? You should probably call ahead…

Alex waves her off.

ALEX: Stop fussing, Phyll! Go get ready, you two.

Exit Phyllis and Andrea. Mark gets up, stretches and sits next to Alex.

MARK: Well done, Dad! You steered Mom away from telling us why she came.

ALEX: I'm an old hand at deviousness.

He grins. Mark is serious.

ALEX: What's the matter with you? You want to know more, don't you? That's why you came.

MARK: Yes. I've been married for a couple of years now, Dad. Living with someone is not easy. There are always going to be differences. It's how you deal with them. It's the choices you make in life.

ALEX: Yes, we make choices. We chose to marry, your mom and I. It was a decision we made. I chose to leave. That was also a decision.

MARK: Choices. That's a word you were fond of. You always said that choice was one of the most powerful things you could have. That the biggest lesson in life was to always keep your options under your control. So you could make the choice and not let anyone else choose for you.

ALEX: I did say that. I still believe it. Things don't happen by themselves. You let them happen.

MARK: Was it that hard to live with Mom?

Alex pauses.

ALEX: I... I think there comes a time when we have to make choices. There's that word again....

MARK: It does keep popping up.

ALEX: You don't think your Mom made choices too? You made choices too, you know. You were old enough to, living alone already. You chose to keep away too.

MARK: Yes, I did make that choice. At first, I think, the shock made me want to go away and think. Then the time went by, things happened, work got in the way.

ALEX: Life. That's what it is called. Life gets in the way. That's what they say. Life. But that's wrong, you know.

MARK: Wrong? How can life be wrong?

ALEX: Life is about having the people you love and the people who love you around you. Life is about them. And you. Together. Sure, you have a life, even when you're alone and away from the ones you love. Is it a life that you would choose?

MARK: But you did. You chose to when you left. One of the reasons I came here was to tell you that you're going to be a grandfather soon.

ALEX: Hey! Congratulations! Phyllis didn't tell me that!

Puts his handout. They shake hands. Alex puts his hand on Mark's shoulder and squeezes it, then draws him into a hug.

MARK: She doesn't know. Neither does Andrea. I found out 2 days ago. By that time, Mom had flown out here and Andrea was having a fit. And I made my choice.

ALEX: I see! That's why you came. But that's not all of it, is it? You really want to know why I left and whether your mom and I are getting back.

MARK: Yes. I know you have no obligation to tell me. But I'd like to know.

ALEX: It's quite odd. All these years have gone by. I haven't asked myself that question for a while now. Yet in the last week, it seems, everyone I meet wants to know that.

MARK: When you make choices, you make choices based on data available. What was the data? Let's assemble the data.

ALEX: Am I in court now?

MARK: Yes. Now, I'm going to ask you some simple questions, so we can get to the truth.

ALEX: There were so many things.

MARK: Let's explore them in order.

ALEX: Hmm. Not sure if there is any order to it.

MARK: Would you say that you felt you were being neglected?

ALEX: Ah, I don't know.

MARK: Yes, you do. You must answer that question. You know the answer. It's a simple yes or no question. Did you feel neglected?

ALEX: Yes.

MARK: Did you feel unloved?

ALEX: Uh... no.

MARK: Did having kids bother you?

ALEX: No.

MARK: Did you think your work was to blame?

ALEX: No.

MARK: So if the kids did not bother you and the work didn't either. Then Mom bothered you. Yes or no?

ALEX: Yes.

MARK: Have you talked to her about it?

ALEX: I tried to...

MARK: Stick to yes / no answers only, please.

ALEX: I did. Yes.

MARK: You tried to? Or did you actually talk to her?

ALEX: I suppose, I tried.

MARK: Ok. So, you say you tried.

ALEX: Yes. I did try.

MARK: Have you told here why you left?

ALEX: She never asked.

MARK: I see. And you never bothered to talk to her, did you say?

ALEX: I said I tried. I told you.

MARK: Did she understand what you said?

ALEX: You'll have to ask her! You're asking for my opinion! Won't do in court, young man!

Mark grins.

MARK: I suppose that's why they haven't let me loose on my own in court so far.

ALEX: But you have been in court, right?

MARK: Oh yes, as one of the background minions assisting the lead. I'm learning a lot, though, just from watching the big guns.

ALEX: It's only a matter of time before they give you your own day in court. They want you to watch and learn for a bit. It'll come soon. Then you better be good and prepared!

MARK: Yeah. You know, I've read your books.

ALEX: And?

MARK: And I'll give you my opinion. I think you still care for Mom and you'd like to get back with her.

ALEX: Opinion! Well, there's the small matter of choice. Her choice.

MARK: Yes, of course. But we can work on that.

He gets up. Alex does too.

ALEX: We?

MARK: Sure! Haven't you always bet on the love of your first-born child?

ALEX: Smart-ass!

MARK: Dad... thanks for everything. I don't think I ever said that. I'm sorry, I should have spoken to you about the wedding.

Alex draws him into a hug. Phyllis enters and stops. Alex draws away, but retains his hand around Mark's shoulder.

ALEX: Hey! Phyll, guess what! Mark has fantastic news! Tell her, Mark.

Andrea enters.

ANDREA: Mark has news?

ALEX & PHYLLIS: Andrea, shush!

MARK: Claire is pregnant. We're going to have a baby.

Phyllis and Andrea squeal. Phyllis hurries over and hugs Mark, followed by Andrea.

ANDREA: When is she due? Will she still be able to be my maid of honour?

Phyllis looks at Alex, who slaps his forehead. Mark makes a face at Andrea.

ACT III - Scene 1

It is evening. Andrea is sitting alone on the couch peering into her phone. Alex comes in.

ALEX: Hey, Andy.

She looks up from her phone and puts it away on the low table in front of her.

ANDREA: I can't believe that you live here by yourself, Dad. It's beautiful.

ALEX: Yeah, I like it too. I love to sit here and look out. Sometimes I bring a book out here, but I always find it hard to read out here. It's so restful somehow that ignoring it with a book seems...

Waves his hands.

ANDREA: I was just checking my messages and ... Dad, I wanted to ask you something.

Sits down next to her.

ALEX: What's up? Something bothering you?

ANDREA: It's just...

ALEX: It's ok, Andy. Your secret is safe with me.

ANDREA: Like old times, huh?

ALEX: Yep. Just like old times. Now tell me what's bugging you.

ANDREA: I....do you feel sometimes that you don't understand people?

ALEX: I don't understand anyone at all. I can barely understand my own brain, forget about others'.

ANDREA: I'm serious, Dad.

ALEX: I know you are. So am I. I'm trying to tell you that it's ok not to understand, that you're not the only one.

ANDREA: That doesn't sound right, Dad.

ALEX: What doesn't sound right?

ANDREA: I mean, you had a pretty good career, good jobs, ran a business, now you've written these books and everyone says how much understanding you show in your writing.

ALEX: So?

ANDREA: I was reading this review by this one lady who said that you show the world what real relationships are about.

Alex chuckles softly.

ALEX: Haven't you learned yet not to read reviews? Look, Andy, look at the view there. Just look at it, take a couple of minutes.

Waits.

ALEX: Now, think. Think about yourself. You grew up with Mom, Mark and I. You went through high school, went to the prom with that spotty kid...

ANDREA: Chet...

ALEX: Chet. Then I went away. You went to college, got your degree. I suppose you had a good time, met some nice people, partied, laughed. There may have been days you cried, too.

She nods, staring in front of her.

ALEX: Then you met Dave. How long have you known him?

ANDREA: 3 years, nearly.

ALEX: Now you're getting married to him. He likes you enough, loves you enough, to want to marry you. That's quite something, don't you think?

ANDREA: That's what worries me. He says he wants to marry me, but he's just no help when it comes to the actual wedding itself. All the planning, he doesn't seem to want it to be perfect. Now...

She tails away. Alex moves closer and puts his arm around her, drawing her close.

ALEX: He doesn't seem worried that you went away for two days... right?

She nods.

ALEX: I'm not going to give you advice and tell you what to do. I'm no expert. When it comes to relationships, there are no experts.

ANDREA: But, Dad...

ALEX: Andy, relationships are about you and that view out there. There's you and there's that view. What you do is up to you. It's your choice. You can look at it briefly and go about doing other things. You can sit here and stare at it for hours. I have. Do you know that as the light changes late in the day, the view also seems to change?

ANDREA: But the view is independent of me, Dad. My husband isn't. He shouldn't be. I mean, he and I are starting a life together. Together. Shouldn't we be more involved with each other?

ALEX: He is not dependent on you, though. And you're not dependent on him. You're independent people. That view is not dependent on you. How you react to each other is up to both of you. It's the choices you make. When you make those choices and things go wrong, don't blame the other for it. Remember, you made the choice.

ANDREA: Is that what happened with you and Mom? Did you blame each other?

ALEX: I think, Andy, that what happened with your Mom and I, was that the choices we made didn't work out as we expected. I don't think either side blames the other. At least, I don't think so.

ANDREA: Mom would never allow us to say anything bad about you, you know. She said pretty much what you just said. "Things didn't work out, the choices we made had results we had not anticipated." She said we should give you some time and space.

Alex nods slowly.

ALEX: Time and space, yup...

ANDREA: Are you happy, Dad? Are you happy you went away? Is this what you wanted?

ALEX: Happiness is a relative thing. People are happier at some times and not so happy at others. There is a good side and bad side to every situation. Is there happiness to be found here? Sure. Are there days you wish you had something else, something more? Sure. Yes, there are always more than two paths you can go on, but in the long run it's the choices you make that define the path you're on. That's what Led Zep actually meant.

ANDREA: Ah. Do you think you still have time to change the road you're on? Would you change it? What else do you want now? What would make you happier?

ALEX: Well, I'm glad to see Mark is all set now, has a good career ahead of him, kid on the way. You're getting married too. There's no value in trying to change what has already happened. Look to the future.

ANDREA: Shall I tell you something? I haven't even told Mom, yet. You know how she gets all freaked out and wants to work things out.

ALEX: Let me guess. Dave has been offered a new role over in this neck of the woods. If he accepts you'll be moving down there, across the valley.

He points. She breaks away from him and jumps up.

ANDREA: You knew! You called him, didn't you? You're horrible!

ALEX: Relax! Sit here.

He indicates the seat next to him.

ALEX: He called me this morning. Contrary to what you think, he was

81

worried about you and wanted to make sure everything was ok. We had a nice chat.

She sits down again, shaking her head.

ANDREA: Men! Can't be trusted...

ALEX: Look at this way. He knows you well and he cares for you. At least he didn't call your mom and tell her.

ANDREA: He's a darling all right! Wait till I get a hold of him! How did he get your number?

ALEX: You left it written down on a pad by the phone. You probably left it there in your rush to get here.

ANDREA: Hmm. Sneaking around my things!

ALEX: All in a good cause, though. He was worried. You know, when you move, we'll be almost neighbours... I will like that.

ANDREA: I'd like that too.

She leans her head on his shoulder.

ANDREA: Don't tell Mom, yet, please.

ALEX: Your secret is safe with me.

ANDREA: Thanks soon-to-be-neighbour!

He puts his arm around her and they sit there as the lights go out.

ACT III - Scene 2

Alex is sitting, legs stretched out, relaxed. Andrea is texting on her phone. Phyllis enters. She walks over to Alex.

PHYLLIS: What are you guys doing? Where's Mark?

Andrea looks up from her phone.

ANDREA: Oh, we were just chatting. Dad was saying how much he misses you, Mom. I'll just leave you guys to chat about that while I go find Mark.

Grabs her phone and hurries out. Alex's smile is short-lived as he sees Phyllis is not amused.

PHYLLIS: What have you been telling her? I don't think we should discuss our issues with the kids.

ALEX: She was just kidding, Phyll. You should know that I wouldn't.

PHYLLIS: We'll have to work out our arrangement.

ALEX: Yes.

PHYLLIS: I can't stay here. I'd have liked to go back with Mark and Andrea. But I can't get seats. I've arranged to fly back day after. I wanted to say thank you for everything.

ALEX: No thanks are necessary. Glad to help, anytime and always. You don't have to go, unless you want to. What time is their flight?

PHYLLIS: We have to be at the airport by 11:30 in the morning.

ALEX: Ok, Plenty of time to have breakfast before we have to head out.

PHYLLIS: Oh, don't worry about that.

ALEX: I'm up pretty early anyway and you know, I'd like to have some coffee and toast before I leave.

PHYLLIS: I'll take a cab and drop them off. Don't bother coming all the way.

ALEX: Phyll, you are not taking them in a cab. I'm driving you guys to the airport.

PHYLLIS: But that little car of yours won't hold all of the luggage and us.

ALEX: I have another one somewhere. You leave that to me. I'm driving them. Phyll. You can cancel that cab.

She stares at him. He stares her down.

PHYLLIS: That just doesn't make any sense. We've already taken too much of your time.

ALEX: There is no need to think about my time. It's quite ok. I will drive them tomorrow.

His voice is cold and flat.

84

PHYLLIS: You're being silly.

ALEX: Well, that's who I am. I am the silliest person you ever met. What time is your flight the day after? I'll drive you too.

PHYLLIS: Oh Alex, it's really not necessary. You have stuff to do, I'm sure.

ALEX: I'm not that busy. I've decided to retire completely.

PHYLLIS: What!

ALEX: You heard me. I'm quitting the game. Once the wedding is over, I'll go away for a bit. I'm selling this place. I think it's best. I really don't need this much room and all this.

He indicates the area around him.

PHYLLIS: It's everything you wanted! You have it now.

ALEX: It's not everything.

PHYLLIS: I get that. But what you do have, are you just going to throw it away? Just like that? And run away? Again? How long will you keep running away?

ALEX: You see it as running away. I don't.

PHYLLIS: You are running away. You won't face up to the situation. That's what you always do. Why won't you ever talk about it?

ALEX: What is there to talk about? We split up. You came here to see me, to get me to attend Andrea's wedding. You have that now. What else is there?

PHYLLIS: What else? You can sit there and say that?

ALEX: Yes. I did just say that. What else is there? You got what you wanted, didn't you?

PHYLLIS: Really? You're so blind, Alex! Is that what you got out of all this?

ALEX: Yes. That's what it looks like to me.

PHYLLIS: What did you expect? That I would just forget and move back into your life? Now, that you're ready to resume? Did you ever consider whether I'm ready?

ALEX: I don't think I asked you for anything when you got here.

PHYLLIS: No. You didn't ask. It just seeps out of every pore of this house. Alex, just because you deal in words doesn't mean everyone else does or has to. Some things are better said without words. You understand that, you feel it but you won't let yourself free.

ALEX: Free? Free from what?

PHYLLIS: You know what I mean. You're not stupid.

ALEX: I'm not? But I feel stupid. You came all the way here and now you're going back.

PHYLLIS: Yes. I have a house out there, remember?

ALEX: Yes. I know. And you're going back to it.

PHYLLIS: Well, what do you want me to do?

ALEX: I'm not going to tell you what to do.

PHYLLIS: Why not? What would you like me to do?

ALEX: Whatever you feel like doing. Do it.

PHYLLIS: Whatever I feel? I can do whatever I feel like doing? Do you mean that, Alex? Really?

ALEX: Yes. I have nothing more to say. You have to do what you want.

PHYLLIS: Or feel, right?

ALEX: Yes. What you feel is what you feel. Follow that feeling.

PHYLLIS: Oh, I see. We're now into feelings. What are you feeling, Alex?

ALEX: I feel that nothing has changed.

PHYLLIS: Do you know how I feel now? How I felt all those years?

ALEX: I think you felt I didn't support you enough.

PHYLLIS: You never had the time for us... me. We needed you then.

ALEX: And now?

PHYLLIS: Now you have the time and we don't need you.

Alex nods, gently.

ALEX: Yes, you don't need me. Now. You didn't need me then, either, did you? No, that's not right. You did need me. You needed me to back up every decision that you made. Your decisions. Now you've realized that you don't need me at all. Not for anything.

PHYLLIS: Alex, Alex, Alex! Stop! Can't you see what you're doing? To yourself? To me? To the kids? The past is gone Alex. It's over. You can't bring it back. You can't live in the past. You cannot create a fantasy and live in it. There's a real world out there, Alex. You're in it. There are people in this world, people who love you and care deeply to see you happy.

ALEX: I see the world. I'm in it, as you said. I can't help seeing it.

PHYLLIS: You don't see! Look at the way Mark and Andrea have taken off where they left off. Mark came all the way to tell you about the baby. He just needed an excuse to get in touch. Don't be hard on him for that. He reached out. That should mean something. Does that sink in somewhere into your head?

Alex sits down heavily.

PHYLLIS: I saw you sitting here with Andrea. I overheard some of the conversation. Do you know she hasn't told me about Dave's offer? You think I didn't know? Dave let it slip when he was over the day before I left. I asked him about how his work was going, while Andy had gone to the powder room.

ALEX: And you never mentioned it to me.

PHYLLIS: Alex, she chose to tell you first. She made that choice. Mark made that choice. They could have called me to ask me what I was doing here so long. She took a plane all the way here to see you in person. And Mark, he came, he says, to support her. Do you think he didn't want to fly here too? Of course they did. They wanted to. They made that choice.

ACT III - SCENE 2

She sits down opposite him.

PHYLLIS: Alex, look up. Look at me, Alex. Look me in the eye.

He looks up, slowly.

PHYLLIS: Did you believe that I needed to fly all the way to ask you to come for the wedding? Do you think that? You know I hate flying alone. You used to say that sending me anywhere was like a moon mission, remember?

ALEX: Yes. I remember that. I said a lot of horrible things. You know that I never meant it to hurt. It was said out of affection.

PHYLLIS: Did you ever stop to think about why I extended my stay?

ALEX: What does it matter now? You're going back the day after.

PHYLLIS: Alex, you fool! You're smart and intelligent in so many ways, but you're an absolute idiot….

ALEX: It doesn't matter, anyway.

PHYLLIS: What doesn't?

ALEX: Everything. It's over. The kids are going back tomorrow, I'll drop them, and they'll go away. You'll go away the day after. I'll come for the wedding and to see Mark's new baby. We'll all go back to our lives. Maybe we'll be in touch more often, though. I'd like that.

PHYLLIS: Alex, stop sniveling. I hate to see you whining. Sit up straight and listen carefully. Are you listening?

Alex sits up.

89

PHYLLIS: Ok. Yes, the kids are going tomorrow. They have to. They both have work and lives to live. Both have new chapters in their lives coming up. They came here hoping you will be there to write those chapters with them. Be a part of their story, for your own good. Just take it as it comes. Go in with low expectations.

He is suddenly alert.

ALEX: And you?

PHYLLIS: I'm leaving the day after. Thank you for a really pleasant stay. I have to admit that I did not expect it to be quite so pleasant. Let's just leave it at that for now, shall we? Let's just get Andrea's wedding done.

ALEX: By then I'll have sold this place. I have to start thinking about where I'll go next.

PHYLLIS: You will do no such thing. You're not going to sell this lovely place. It's your dream home. What an absolutely foolish thing to do! You really are a fool, Alex. A very foolish romantic. What did you have in mind? A trip up the Amazon to forget your unrequited love? You're not a hero in one of those early 20th century novels. You're barely any kind of hero at all.

ALEX: But…

PHYLLIS: Promise me you won't.

ALEX: Why?

PHYLLIS: Promise, Alex!

ALEX: I don't know.

PHYLLIS: I need that promise!

ALEX: Oh man! Whatever! Ok, I promise.

PHYLLIS: Good boy! Now, let's get the kids for our last dinner here before we all go back to where we were before.

She gets up and walks behind him and puts her hand on his head.

ALEX: The way we were before?

Smacks him gently on his head then grabs him by the hair and gives it a gentle shake.

PHYLLIS: When will you learn, Alex? When will you start trusting your heart and stop worrying about making the right choice every time?

ACT III - Scene 3

Two months later. Alex and Linda enter.

Alex is dressed in jeans, loafers and a shirt, Linda in a business suit.

ALEX: Yes, it went off without a hitch.

LINDA: So your kids are both married now, you're going to be a grandfather soon. What's next?

ALEX: Nothing much. It's the same old, same old. I write, you make me do it over, Stephanie fixes the typos, the grammar mistakes and points out the rubbishy bits, I fix it, you take it away and sell it. We both get paid.

He's about to say something, but stops himself. He sits down in the left hand side chair and waves her to the sofa.

She sits down.

LINDA: Tell me about the wedding! You were gone an awful long time! The wedding didn't take that long so what were you up to?

ALEX: I went a week ahead. Andrea wanted me to. The wedding itself took a couple of days. Paul and Janet, Dave's parents, had a big reception the next day. So it was two whole days of drinking, dancing, meeting people.

LINDA: Met some old friends?

ALEX: I did. Mixed bag, really.

LINDA: You've been away a long time. Give me details! Where did you stay? With Phyllis?

ALEX: You are the world's worst nosey-parker! You should have come, you were invited, you know.

LINDA: Very kind of you, thanks! I couldn't. I had to arm-wrestle a few people.

ALEX: I see. Business before pleasure. Money before curiosity.

LINDA: OK, so you know me well. So give! Tell me more!

ALEX: Well, I flew over early, as I said. To help out with the prep.

LINDA: Huh! You helped?

ALEX: Well, I did have great ideas. But they seemed to have it all laid out.

LINDA: And how did it go with Phyllis?

ALEX: Nice house, she has there.

LINDA: Did you or did you not stay in Phyllis' house?

ALEX: Well, you know a hotel for 6 weeks would have been ruinously expensive.

LINDA: Ah. Yes. Of course! Silly me!

ALEX: Yes. It was a good few weeks, actually.

LINDA: It was, huh?

ALEX: Yeah. The wedding kept us quite busy.

LINDA: The wedding kept you busy, huh? How was the wedding?

ALEX: The usual thing. You meet all kinds of people, some old friends. Everyone's busy with their own thing.

LINDA: Meeting old friends is always a hit or miss affair.

ALEX: Yeah. I found that some of them didn't really care to know more about me. They've gone on with their lives.

LINDA: Hmm. But there must have been some who would have been happy to meet a well-known author.

ALEX: There were the folks who were mildly curious, of course. Some had even heard I had written a book. There was a couple who had even read one or two of them.

Linda leans back and shakes her head.

LINDA: You are a cynical, horrible beast of a man. I'm not sure what I find likeable about you. The sad thing is you are likeable.

ALEX: It's your fatal flaw, Linda. You are a cynic-lover.

LINDA: I guess I am.

ALEX: Warped! That's what you are.

LINDA: I am. It's all that hobnobbing with emotionally fragile writer types.

ALEX: You and I, we're both the same; warped and cynical. And we're the sane ones, we think. What hope is there for this world?

LINDA: None whatsoever. So what did you and Phyllis decide?

ALEX: Well, she has one child out there and another here. I suppose she will be travelling a bit.

LINDA: I see. And what do you have in mind?

ALEX: Me? Much of a muchness, really. Same routine.

LINDA: I see, basic boring stuff, huh?

ALEX: Yeah.

LINDA: You're staying on here?

ALEX: I guess so. I'm starting to like this place. Besides, she made me promise I wouldn't move.

LINDA: I see. She made you promise; she being Phyllis, right? And you didn't like this before?

ALEX: Hmm. Yes. I did like this before. Or maybe, I didn't. Maybe, it's the promise….I have no idea what I'm saying anymore.

LINDA: Oh my god! What date is it? I have to mark this as the day you confessed to babbling incoherently.

ALEX: Funny. Ha ha.

LINDA: So what happens next?

ALEX: Nothing. Life goes on. There will be some changes, I suppose, now that I seem to have gained a couple of kids-in-law and a grandchild.

LINDA: I see.

ALEX: You do?

LINDA: Yes. When is she coming here next?

ALEX: Soon, I suppose. Who knows?

LINDA: You really are an infuriating man.

ALEX: Am I?

LINDA: Yes. You are. But, there is a silver lining.

ALEX: Oh, is there?

LINDA: Yes, the world wants us to give them more of your work. So where is the new manuscript!

ALEX: And you have the gall to call me a cynical beast! Man, do you think of nothing else but your business? Have you no soul?

LINDA: Nope! Business is business, Al, my friend. You said it earlier. Business before pleasure.

ALEX: And I was right.

LINDA: I say it differently. Business is pleasure.

ALEX: You do this for pleasure?

LINDA: Yep. Now, my man, let's talk about that manuscript you owe me.

ALEX: Do you harangue all your writers the same way? They must all love you very much.

LINDA: You're the only one I deal with personally. All the others have to make do with members of my staff.

ALEX: Wow! I don't know whether to feel honoured or threatened. Either way, I'm left with little choice but to give in to you.

He walks over to the door of his office and pulls it open. She stares at him.

LINDA: In there? We never go in there! What has happened to you?

She gets up slowly. He stands at the door, his hand on the door-handle, waiting for her. She tip-toes in. He moves behind his desk and sits down and waves Linda to the visitor's chair.

She stands across the table, eyes closed and hands out, in a meditative pose.

LINDA: Hmm...

ALEX: Now what?

LINDA: Shhhh!

ALEX: Take your time. I have all day, you know. I live here. I don't have to go anywhere.

LINDA: Hush! Stop talking. I want to absorb the hallowed air of this ... this...

this…

Snaps her fingers.

ALEX: Room?

LINDA: Nope!

ALEX: Office?

LINDA: Oh no.

ALEX: Den?

LINDA: Umm… no

ALEX: Workspace?

LINDA: Nah.

ALEX: Studio?

LINDA: No… wait! Haven? No. That's not quite it. Bunker! Yes, this bunker.

She opens her eyes and looks around the room. She makes a careful inspection of the bookshelves. She walks over to check out the watercolours on the walls.

Alex sits there watching her. She comes up against the chair in the corner to Alex's left.

She stops and turns around to look at him. She shakes her head.

LINDA: So you're not a cynical beast, after all, are you? You're a softie! I was right all along!

Alex shrugs.

ALEX: I am whatever they say I am. So, she told you, eh?

Linda moves back around the table and stands by his side.

LINDA: Yes Alex. She told me and I'd always suspected it, anyway. Thanks for confirming my suspicions.

She draws a deep breath and puts her hand on his shoulder.

LINDA: So, what do we do now?

ALEX: Well, there're always a couple of choices. We could sit down and go over the plans for the new book or you could go away and leave me to get on with my life.

LINDA: You know, I'm going to go away.

ALEX: What?

LINDA: This … This is too much to take.

She waves her hand around the room.

ALEX: Try not to get those Victorian style vapours.

LINDA: Quiet, Alex!

ALEX: I'm sorry, Linda. I really am. You've been a very good friend when I really needed one. I will never forget that. Never.

LINDA: I won't let you! Always remember one thing.

ALEX: What?

LINDA: I won't wait forever. For that book! It's in the contract. So, Al, my friend, you don't have a choice anymore. Better get on it right away.

ALEX: I don't have a choice. One more book, Linda. It's in the contract. After that I have more than a couple of choices.

LINDA: Are you going to quit writing?

ALEX: I'm exploring the options in front of me.

LINDA: I see. You want a new contract, don't you?

ALEX: Well, there's this vineyard…

She cuts him off.

LINDA: Listen, get this one done. We can talk. I'd hate to let you go. We can explore those choices, always. Get this one done first! OK?

ALEX: No choice there, is that it?

LINDA: None, whatsoever! You better get to work, mister.

ALEX: Ok! I have to do some thinking, then.

He gets up and comes around to face her. They stare at each other. She gives him a hug, before moving back to the door.

LINDA: Stay well, my friend. Let me know when you're done, ok?

ALEX: Will you let yourself out, so I can start on my thinking?

LINDA: Yes. I always let myself out, remember?

He walks over to the chair in the corner, and throws himself into it and stretches out. He closes his eyes and lies there.

Linda stares at him, shakes her head, and walks away out to the patio and exits via the kitchen door.

The lights fade on Alex lying there with his eyes closed.

~~~~~

Note from the Author

Thank you for reading this far.

I do hope you like the story in this book. I'd be delighted to hear from you, whether you liked it or not.

If you do decide to leave a review, please do be frank. I would love to know what you liked, and what you didn't like is just as important to me. Don't just make polite noises.

Do take a look at "Uncommon Pie & Other Stories", out now in paperback and ebook format. It features a collection of stories to thrill, chill and make you chuckle.

I do release small snippets and samples on my website, www.sloword.com, from time to time, together with other essays, articles, recipes and travelogues. You may wish to check it out.

Thank you,

Ajesh Sharma

2024

About the Author

Ajesh Sharma started writing stories late in life. Some of his short stories have appeared in magazines. He has a number of novels awaiting completion.

A Couple of Choices is his first play.

He uses his blog, sloword.com, to showcase his work.

When not wearing colourful socks or attempting to play guitar, he tries to read, write, learn photography and spend time with his family on the outskirts of Toronto, Canada.

You can connect with me on:

🌐 https://www.sloword.com

www.ingramcontent.com/pod-product-compliance
Lightning Source LLC
Chambersburg PA
CBHW030555130626
46552CB00006B/2550